DR. FUDDLE AND THE
GOLD BATON

DR. FUDDLE AND THE GOLD BATON

Warren L. Woodruff

Story Merchant Books
Beverly Hills
2012

Story Merchant Books
9601 Wilshire Boulevard #1202
Beverly Hills CA 90210
www.storymerchant.com/books.html

PRELUDE

High on his cloud-shrouded tower upon a bleak mountain-top stood a royal-looking figure faintly lit by the crescent moon. But a king this was not. His black cape billowed, casting a menacing shadow. An occasional glimpse of a bony wing appeared amidst the folds of red satin lining. He peered out over the mountains and valleys, relishing the sight of darkness and the atmosphere of fear over the land. If he could banish the moon as well, he would.

A small musical sound behind him caught his attention, drawing him back inside his chambers. He stopped at an antique table holding a large *carillons à musique*, his treasured nineteenth-century music box. This was no ordinary music box. His fingers caressed the ebony roses gilding the mechanical instrument. When he lifted the ornate cover, the box played an eerie metallic tune. A smoke-like mist rose from its mirrored interior and from the mist round shapes took form. He stared at the expanding sound bubbles that were forming images before him. A moving picture came into focus inside one of the bubbles:

He watched a blonde boy with blue eyes walk down a street

5

lined with oak trees then bound up the steps into his New England Colonial home. The house was brimming with music and happiness as the boy's mother played the piano and his young sister listened joyfully. Their reserved father sat in his favorite chair lost in reading the newspaper.

The scene in the bubble grew clearer. "Isn't that a sweet scene?" mocked the dark one. "But why is this being shown to me?" Two others stood in the shadows behind him viewing the images, not daring to say a word.

The orbs of sound wobbled. The picture changed as time moved forward. The colonial home had grown dark and the music had stopped. Upstairs in the master bedroom, the boy was sitting in a chair beside his mother's bed, his head buried in the crook of his arm, and clasping her limp hand in his. In the doorway, the little sister clung to their father.

"Ah, so sad, so sad," said the cloaked one in a whisper, studying the boy with interest. "But I don't understand, why are these people being shown to me?"

The boy turned as if he could hear the question from far, far away. Without warning, a blazing light radiated from the music box, sending the dark one reeling. He clutched his chest and struggled to close the lid to shut away the light. His voice turned menacing, "Now I see...I see... You are the one I must prepare for."

Chapter One

Now that he was half past twelve years, Tyler Harrington knew it was time he stopped acting like a frightened child over every little sound in the night or from the blackness of his bedroom, or every time he saw a star disappear, or the millions of other scary notions that crept into his brain. He never used to be that way. And so on this dark evening as he walked home from his friend's, he decided to confront one of his fears. This time he wasn't going to walk several blocks out of the way to avoid the mysterious old house—if you'd call something that huge a house. The rundown manor loomed high on Willow Street Hill, as though keeping a watchful eye on the residents of his quaint New England town. It always sent shivers down his spine and tonight it seemed even more creepy than usual.

Just a few more steps, Tyler thought to himself, *I'm almost past it*. The growing shadows spooked him.

He quickened his pace and remembered the time many years ago when the stars filled the sky. He asked his mother about the old mansion and his father had immediately changed the subject to what they'd be having for dinner.

"We don't want to scare the boy," he'd whispered.

Tyler passed the damp, moss-covered trees that framed the arched windows facing the street. He imagined eyes peering at him from behind the fancy glass, even though as far as he knew, the house had been vacant for decades. He jumped and his heart pounded when a dog howled in the distance.

"One, two, three, four...I can do this!" he counted rhythmically with the next few steps. Tyler found that counting out loud made things easier when he was afraid. Whatever was scaring him might just go away by the time he got to ten. Or at least it helped him keep his mind off scary things until he mustered up enough nerve to open his eyes again.

Then quite suddenly all thoughts of counting flew out of Tyler's mind when he heard something. He stood still and listened, but decided his mind had to be playing tricks on him.

But as soon as he took another step, he heard it again, this time more clearly. The sound was unmistakable. It was piano music.

Surely it must be coming from another house, he thought. He moved closer to listen more carefully, but then stopped dead in his tracks. He knew the melody very well. It was the special Beethoven tune his mother had played for his mute little sister, Christina. It was Christina's favorite music.

Their mother was a highly respected piano teacher throughout her lifetime. So many people, usually grown-ups, had exclaimed, "How fortunate you are to have such a wonderful music instructor in your very own house," knowing full well he didn't take piano lessons. He didn't know why he'd resisted music lessons all these years, he just had. Music wasn't for him. He was thankful his mother hadn't forced him, like so many parents did. His friend Kathy had to take lessons with his mom and she would drag herself over to his house every week. He could tell her heart wasn't in it because it showed in her mechanical playing. She put on the image of "culture" the same way she put on her designer clothes.

It was getting darker and Tyler really didn't want to get any closer to the mansion. But the tune was so peppy and full of energy, like a little dog chasing its tail, so familiar, that it seemed to be calling to him. Hearing it filled his mind with memories. He thought of how Christina danced to that music and how their mother promised she'd teach her how to play it some day when she was older. Unfortunately that day never came. Their mother was gone from this world and for the last two years Tyler and Christina lived with their no-nonsense father, the Honorable Judge Harrington, and the live-in nanny.

Tyler was finally learning to accept his family's new situation, but he could never forget the last night with his mother before she passed on.

In her fitful sleep, she'd awakened from a dark vision of future destruction. The nightmare terrified her, but hope lingered in her eyes when she spoke. "Tyler, dear, someday you'll be doing something very important—something wonderful for Christina and yourself and for many others. I'll send you a clear sign when it's time. A great teacher will guide you."

Tyler had clung to that hope, looking high and low for the sign, but two years had passed and nothing remarkable had happened. He was beginning to lose faith.

Until now.

Tyler's curiosity overrode any fears or thoughts that he could get himself in a lot of trouble for trespassing onto the grounds of the manor. *One, two, three...am I out of my mind for doing this?* he thought, not sure if he may have actually said the words aloud. *I'm even talking to myself like a crazy person!* He reached the stained glass windows and peered through a gold pane.

The unmistakable feeling of being watched turned his skin icy cold. He looked around but saw no one peering at him from the shadows. When he looked back through the gold glass, what he saw made his hair stand on end.

A man sat at an enormous grand piano—but this man was like none he'd ever seen. Tyler could see right through him. The man's hazy fingers moved easily and rapidly over the keys, and beyond his wispy figure shone a mystifying light, with strangely dressed people disappearing in and out of it. The man turned his head toward Tyler.

Tyler wanted to capture evidence to prove to himself he wasn't dreaming, so he pulled out his cell phone. But just as he started to video-record the scene the music stopped abruptly. The man disappeared into thin air and the oddly dressed people were swallowed into the wall.

Everything went dark.

Tyler knew beyond any doubt this had to be his mother's long-awaited sign and he ran home as fast as his feet could carry him, counting every step.

CHAPTER TWO

When he climbed into bed, Tyler dreamed about Christina's tune calling to him, but soon his dreams turned into the most bizarre nightmares he'd ever had; he was wandering through dark tunnels and running from creatures of all shapes and sizes.

When daylight finally broke, Tyler welcomed being jolted back to reality. *Only dreams* he silently assured himself. He rubbed his eyes and looked around his room, comforted by the familiar poster of the solar system and pictures of remote castles he'd hung on the walls, pictures that had belonged to his grandfather. Tyler had never been interested in the things that interested other boys his age.

He headed straight downstairs and found Christina playing a game with Dolly. Since being parted from her mother, Christina and her doll were always together. In her favorite floral dresses, Christina almost looked like her old-fashioned doll. Her hair was blonde like her brother's, and hung gracefully in long waves. Their father the judge had already set off to work for a day at court. Their nanny was humming to herself while tidying up the house.

"You want to go on an adventure, Christina?"

She hopped up, eyes sparkling.

"One last time before school starts next week!" He took her hand and they raced out the door while he shouted to their nanny, "We'll be back soon!" He looked down at his sister, "But we've got to find Antonio first."

They didn't even notice that the sky had grown overcast as they turned down Elm Street. Tyler could see Antonio standing outside with a group of boys near an open garage down the street. They shared the same birthday and felt like non-identical twins, though Antonio looked much older. Compared to Tyler, Antonio was athletically built. Things turned lively whenever Antonio arrived on the scene with his striking good looks and ready-for-anything attitude. Lately, though, he was going through a rebellious, spiked hair stage and hanging out with guys very unlike Tyler, which was exactly what he was doing at the moment.

As Tyler and Christina approached, Christina covered her ears at the sound of wild behavior and harsh music coming from an amateur band in the garage. Tyler grasped her hand and regretted bringing her here.

"Hey, Antonio, what's up?" Tyler asked. The music stopped. Several boys snickered at the sight of the wholesome-looking boy and his little sister holding his hand.

Antonio smiled at Tyler and Christina. "Hey, Tyler!" he said. "I didn't expect to see you here!"

"Tell them to get lost," a rough voice yelled.

"Knock it off," Antonio said. "They're my friends."

Tyler was proud to be Antonio's friend, knowing sticking up for them wasn't the easy thing to do. But what he didn't understand was why Antonio wanted to hang out with these guys, especially since they seemed to be getting meaner lately and turning into bullies. A couple of them had even been suspended from school.

"It's happened!" Tyler said.

"What's happened?"

The biggest of the boys in the garage came out. He leered at Antonio and said in a fake sing-songy voice, "Why don't you just run along now and play with your little friends? Maybe you can play a game with the girlie who can't talk and her freaky little doll." The other boys laughed.

Tyler glared at them, picking Christina up and wiping away her tears.

"I told you to knock it off!" Antonio said, leaning into the bully's face.

"You'll never be good enough to stay in our band anyway," the bully snickered and walked back into the garage.

Antonio looked stricken.

"He's better than you'll ever be!" Tyler yelled. "Come on, Christina, don't pay any attention to these jerks." Before turning away he said to Antonio, "I've got something very important to tell you, Tony."

"Can it wait until later?" Antonio replied.

Tyler frowned. "How much later?"

"How about tonight around seven?"

"I guess that'll work," Tyler replied, lowering his voice. "What's this all about?"

"You'll find out soon enough. Just meet us at seven o'clock sharp at the corner of Oak and Willow."

"Okay, see you then." Antonio wanted to hug Christina, but decided against it knowing his new friends were watching him.

Tyler stalked off with his sister, his face turning red upon hearing more rude remarks. When they were out of sight, Christina reached for her brother's hand.

They walked down the maple-lined streets of their quaint town, enjoying the last sights and smells of summer and feeling the first hints of fall. Christina skipped over to the park, dragging him to the swings. Tyler pushed her high up into the air, her flowery dress swirling behind her, his laughter blowing away the sadness with the breeze.

The day dragged by but when seven o'clock finally came, they reached the corner of Oak and Willow, and found Antonio was already there. It was growing dark quickly. The life-long friends greeted each other with their usual secret handshake. "Sorry we showed up this morning without telling you. It won't happen again," Tyler said.

Antonio shrugged. "Don't worry about it, Ty. Hey, hope you don't mind, but I invited Kathy and Leonard."

"Why'd you do that?" Tyler said with a frown. Kathy and Leonard were two of their closest friends, but he'd really not wanted to include them this time. He knew they'd never believe him about what he'd seen and heard the night before.

"I don't know," Antonio said. "You looked like there was something exciting going on and I thought they'd want in on whatever it is. We've always done everything together."

Kathy and Leonard walked up, greeting them. Both looked older than their thirteen years. Kathy Goldman was attractive with auburn hair, brown eyes framed with fashionable glasses, fine features and had style to burn, always sporting the latest trendy clothes. Her mother owned a designer ladies' clothing store and her father was a leading surgeon.

Leonard Lang, son of a renowned award-winning bio-chemist from China, was super-intelligent and offbeat, yet shared his father's genes that demanded scientific proof of all things. He liked being with Kathy and knew there was more to her than her obsession with fashion. He admired her technical ability on the piano. He had always thought he might like to give music a try. The mathematical precision of it stirred his curiosity; but he just hadn't found the time with all his science fairs and clubs. "So what's the urgency?" Leonard asked, with a hint of irritation.

14

"Just come on," Tyler answered, leading them up the street.

Kathy followed, thinking how Tyler should rid himself of his dull, preppy image, maybe grow his hair a little longer.

Tyler halted when they stood directly across from the mansion.

"Why are we stopping here?" Kathy asked, staring at the imposing structure set back from the street up on its hill.

The mansion loomed above them with its dozens of arched stained glass windows, topped by a stately dome jutting eighty feet from the ground. A darkened sky stood behind it.

"I thought you avoided this block like the plague!" Leonard said.

"That was before last night. I've always had a strange feeling about this place, like it was haunted, but now I know. Come on," Tyler ordered. "The coast is clear! Follow me."

They followed him grudgingly up the long driveway toward the house passing gothic-looking statues along the way. Kathy brushed autumn leaves off her new fall outfit as she strutted along.

"I heard something strange coming from this place last night at just about this time," Tyler said.

"Are you out of your mind?" Kathy snapped. "You know no one lives here. No one has in ages."

Leonard nudged her and whispered, "Humor him, Kath. He needs us since...well, you know when."

When Leonard spoke in his firm voice, she always melted. "I guess you're right. This is the first time he's been excited about anything in such a long time."

"That's more like it." Leonard grinned and squeezed her arm.

"I heard music coming from here," Tyler said, pushing his way through the bushes toward the window.

Kathy rolled her eyes.

15

"What kind of music?" Antonio asked.

Tyler smiled because he knew Antonio would give him the benefit of the doubt.

He stopped and stooped down by his sister, holding her shoulders gently, staring into her eyes, "Christina, you remember that Beethoven tune Mom played for you so often?" She nodded, grabbed the pad and pencil always in her pocket, and printed, "Rage Over a Lost Penny."

"Well, technically it's called *Rondo e Capriccio*," Kathy corrected. They looked at her in amazement. "Well, I did learn *something* from your mother with all those lessons." Leonard gave her a thumb's up. She blushed.

"Right!" Tyler said. "Well, that's exactly what I heard coming from this room. This is the sign—you know—*the sign*! It's what we've been waiting for."

Christina knew exactly what he was talking about.

And so did the others. They'd been hearing about it for two years.

"Oh, get real, Tyler." Kathy said, trying not to lose her patience. She had huge respect for Tyler's mother and had been one of her most faithful piano students. But Kathy was a no-nonsense person. "You must have imagined the whole thing."

"Don't get her hopes up without proof first, Tyler," Leonard said. "Think, man."

"Yeah, Tyler, chill a little," Antonio said softly, glancing at Christina.

"Look in this window," Tyler said. "What do you see?"

Antonio was the first to peer into the window. "I don't see anything, Tyler. It's too dark in there."

Tyler cupped his hands and looked through the glass. "It wasn't like this last night. There was a strange light and I could see right in."

Leonard looked next. "Nope. Sorry Tyler, but it's just what I expected. Nothing."

Kathy refused to look in the window. "This is absurd," she said and gestured for everyone to follow her away from the house.

"And get this," Tyler paused for effect. "Almost no one knew about the little ending Mom added just for Christina. Remember, Chrissy? I'm no singer, but it went like..." He hummed the ending of the tune, adding their mother's extra chords.

Christina nodded with excitement. She remembered it clearly.

"Well," Tyler continued for the benefit of the others, "those extra chords were being played last night. It *had* to be the sign from Mom."

Dead silence greeted his words. Christina jumped up and down with joy and hugged her brother.

Leonard rubbed his chin in thought. Kathy looked at him wondering if he was convinced, but Antonio stood with his hands on his hips.

"I think we should see if there's a way in," Antonio said, walking over to stand beside Tyler, who shuddered at the thought of entering the dark manor.

"Are you out of your mind? We can't go in there. That's criminal trespassing!" Kathy scolded. "Besides, I heard there was a murder in there a long time ago."

"That's just a rumor," Leonard replied.

"Maybe there're a few ghosts having a party in there besides Mrs. Harrington," Antonio added, just to annoy Kathy. "No disrespect intended, Tyler."

"Well, as a matter of fact," Tyler began, "now that you mention it..."

"Oh great!" Kathy said. "*Now* you're going to tell us you've seen ghosts, too?"

17

"I did," Tyler said, getting up enough nerve to tell the rest of his story. "I saw a man sitting at a grand piano playing Mom's special piece. And I could see through him. But there were others, too, dressed from a long time ago, really old-fashioned."

"I'm out of here!" Kathy shouted, making a beeline for the driveway.

Leonard went after her and ushered her back to the others.

"Stop worrying, Kathy," he said. "Besides there's probably no way to get in. And even if there is, let's check it out. I want to prove to everyone once and for all there's no such thing as ghosts."

The dark, overcast sky hovered thicker and blacker above the deserted street. The friends followed Tyler and Antonio around the corner up onto the back porch. "No one will ever know we're doing this except us," Tyler said. He shivered, thinking of the hundreds of old stories about this mansion—the kind of scary stories grandmothers told from their front porches on dark summer nights when there was nothing else to do. But of course, he didn't let on to the others that he was afraid.

Antonio tried to open the back door, but it was locked.

"Okay, see?" Kathy said. "It's getting late. Time to go home."

A strong gust of wind blew through the keyhole and they all heard a tiny click. Antonio tried the ornate doorknob again and this time the door sprang open.

"Hey, it opened—just for us. Let's go in," Tyler said excitedly.

"You must be joking!" Kathy screeched. "Some hobo could be camping out in there waiting to kill us! Let's get out of here!"

Chapter Three

Kathy looked at her watch. "It's 7:15 already. I've got to get home." She turned to lead Christina away and grabbed her hand, leading her down the porch steps, while Tyler pushed his way into the dark mansion followed by Antonio and Leonard.

"Bring her back, Kathy" Tyler yelled. Suddenly there was a deafening crack of thunder and Christina fled Kathy's grip to run to her brother's side. A heavy downpour gave Kathy no choice but to go back up the steps and join the others. She reluctantly stepped inside but stood close to Leonard.

Together they walked into a large, dark foyer with an arched hallway beyond.

"You *know* what'll happen if we get caught in here?" Kathy's voice echoed off the ceiling. "We'll be grounded for years or worse! There's no telling what kind of trouble we'll be in!"

Tyler tried to ignore Kathy but she persisted, her pitch growing shriller by the second.

"Is anyone listening to me?" She stomped her designer boot.

Christina reached for her brother's hand; they were united in their purpose.

"I don't see any harm done if we're in here just until the rain lets up," Tyler said. He proceeded a few steps into the hallway. His instincts told him it led to where he'd heard the music.

To everyone's amazement, a pleasant scent drifted in their direction, not at all the musty odor they'd expected in a house this old. It smelled very fresh—an outdoorsy, floral kind of aroma—although no flowers were in sight. For the next few moments no one moved or said a word. They huddled together in the dark, listening to the rain outside, when to their complete surprise fancy crystal sconces began to light the tapestry-covered walls along the corridor as far as they could see.

"Holy cow! What is all this stuff?" Antonio asked, shocked at what he saw.

Never in any of their lives had they witnessed such a sight. They found themselves in a seemingly endless hallway. Hanging beside the tapestries were formal portraits of musicians throughout history, captured in oils with their trusty instruments. Busts of famous musicians on pedestals lined the long corridor.

"Obviously *someone important* has moved in here!" Kathy whispered. "I don't care how soaked we get. Let's go! Now!" She stood practically on top of Leonard.

"Kathy's right, you guys," Leonard said. "We've got to get out of here."

"Hello? Is anyone home?" Antonio yelled.

Silence responded.

Tyler put a protective arm around his sister. "Don't be scared, Christina." He turned toward his friends, "Come on you guys, we'll be okay. Let's just look around. I know there's a reason we're supposed to be here."

Leonard grinned. "Yeah, as in to stir up excitement in this dusty old town with tomorrow's headlines reading 'Young hoodlums arrested for breaking and entering!'" He looked at Kathy's frightened face and said, "Don't worry, I'm sure we'll be fine."

"But what if something awful happens in here?" Kathy whispered.

"Don't be so dramatic," Tyler said. "Just look at this place. Could you ever imagine it would be so amazing? Maybe it's been like this for centuries."

Christina looked up at Tyler and smiled. Her calmness eased Tyler's fears.

"Okay, I'll stay a few more minutes," Kathy said. "But I'm warning you guys..."

"C'mon, follow me." Tyler walked softly down the hallway, sensing no one else was in the house. His control of his anxiety surprised even himself. He tried not to think of the trouble he'd be in if he got caught trespassing with his father being the town's only judge.

Slowly but surely they followed him down the corridor, Kathy clutching Leonard's arm.

Antonio stopped and picked up a strange-looking stringed instrument from a shelf. "Get a load of this! What is it? Some kind of guitar?"

"Put that down!" Kathy demanded. "It's a mandolin, you ninny. We are so not supposed to be in here. What's in this place is worth a fortune. Don't touch anything and I mean it! Do you hear me?"

"What's your problem, Kathy?" he yelled back.

"Haven't your parents taught *you* anything? You can't bother other people's belongings!"

"Haven't *your* parents taught you anything? You're in here, too!"

"Cut it out, you two," Tyler demanded.

"Who put you in charge?" Kathy asked.

"I did!" Tyler replied.

When Antonio replaced the relic a musical note exploded through the hallway. Everyone froze. Tyler grabbed Christina and stood with his mouth hanging open. Leonard looked up, trying to figure out the origin of the sound. Kathy covered her mouth to muffle a full blown scream.

"What the..." Antonio croaked, eyes bulging, "...this place *must* be haunted!"

Only Christina seemed completely unfazed by the sound. As a matter of fact, Tyler could've sworn he saw a smile on his sister's lips, her expression hinted that she'd heard the sound before. It was definitely a vocal sound—just one long unfamiliar note followed by stillness.

"Let's stay calm, everyone," Leonard said. A few seconds passed. No one spoke.

Kathy shook uncontrollably and her knees began to knock. She was on the verge of tears. "I'm really scared," she said, looking at Leonard.

Christina smiled and offered Kathy her doll.

"No, that's okay, Christina. You hold onto Dolly."

Leonard turned to examine an oil painting. "Look at this. How interesting."

"Interesting?!" replied Kathy. "How can you say that at a time like this?!"

Tyler and Christina joined Leonard to look at the painting of a man with long, curly black hair and blazing eyes. His formal, dark clothing reflected his bygone era.

"He looks nuts," Kathy said, walking away from the painting. "That's the face of insanity if I ever saw it. Come on, Leonard! Let's leave!"

Antonio touched the painting and jumped back as loud

voices pierced the air accompanied by a flash of lightning and a violent clap of thunder. The entire mansion rocked while *pop, pop, pop!* the hall lights blacked out one by one.

Kathy let out a blood-curdling scream.

Leonard groped through the dark to put his hand over her mouth when Tyler suddenly realized Christina had let go of him.

"Christina! Christina!" he pleaded. The final echoes of Kathy's scream faded into the darkness. He tried not to panic. "Christina, come here, follow my voice!"

After a few miserable seconds, Tyler felt Christina's hand embrace his. A dead calm returned once more. For several long, bone-chilling moments no one moved in the darkness. Suddenly, one by one, the wall chandeliers switched back on, making odd little musical rings as they relit. When the last one came on, everyone looked at each other, puzzled.

Leonard stepped forward. "All right, everyone," he said, attempting to regain his wits. "There's a rational explanation for everything. Besides the fact that we *definitely* shouldn't have come in here, there remains the fact that all this is explainable. We've obviously set off an alarm system meant to deter intruders."

"What are you talking about?!" Kathy yelled. "We have to get out of here! NOW!" She hammered her fist into her palm. Her purse nearly fell to the floor.

"From what I know already," continued Leonard, looking in all directions for cameras and alarms, "someone extremely rich must have bought this house without anyone knowing. They've got this place rigged up with the latest electronic wizardry. We've been caught in the act. They're going to watch every move we make. *They may be watching now.*"

"So what should we do?" Antonio said.

"What should we do? *WHAT SHOULD WE DO?!*" Kathy

repeated hysterically. "For starters *GET OUT OF HERE IMMEDIATELY!*" she ordered, terrified. "Then we'll apologize to the owner of this house and pray he doesn't call the police. This was a *huge* mistake and I knew it all along! Oh why, oh why, OH WHY didn't I trust my judgment? We're in such trouble!"

"Let's just at least try to find the room where I heard that music coming from," Tyler said.

"I agree," Antonio said.

"This stupid adventure has got to end!" Kathy ordered.

"NO!" Tyler shouted.

A sudden cold draft wisped down the hallway, silencing their voices until Antonio said, "Did you feel that?"

"Yeah," Leonard admitted. "Strange, like something just brushed past us."

Kathy stormed down the hallway, but stopped dead in her tracks, staring in disbelief. "It's GONE! The door is gone!"

"She's right!" Antonio looked behind the painting that was now hanging on a wall where the door had stood only moments ago. "It's a solid wall. How could that be? We just *came* through that door! I think we've got more to worry about than being in trouble with our parents or the law."

Leonard didn't say a word.

Christina pointed at the far end of the hallway with a look of terror in her eyes.

"What do you see Christina?" Tyler said. "I don't see anything, do you, Tony?"

Antonio shook his head no. "What is it, Christina?"

She reached into her pocket, scribbling wildly on her pad. Her hands shook. Tyler showed it to the rest of them. On her pad was a black-caped dark figure.

"She saw that in here?!" Antonio asked.

Kathy clutched Leonard's arm. Leonard looked closer at

her drawing. "She's scared. It's just her imagination, that's all."

But Kathy, by this time, was out of her mind. She plowed right into one of the pedestals, hurling a bust of an ancient looking man into the air. Just in the nick of time Leonard caught it before it crashed to the floor. At the very instant they heaved it back onto the pedestal the sounds of a cathedral chorus roared through the corridor. The lights flickered once more.

Before their eyes, Christina rose three feet into the air and stayed suspended in the middle of the hallway. Her eyes were wide, more curious than frightened.

They stared at her, dumbfounded.

"What's the scientific explanation for THAT, Einstein?" Kathy demanded, looking at Leonard.

Leonard glared at her.

Tyler tried to help Christina down, but couldn't budge her. After several minutes, she floated back down to the floor, a little smile played on the corners of her mouth. Tyler grabbed onto her and held her tightly. "Okay, agreed. No question about it, we've got to get out of here."

Leonard looked at Christina standing solidly on the floor. "Don't you see? Our minds are playing tricks on us."

"But you saw her caught in the air as clearly as we did!" Antonio said.

"I'm telling you we're just imagining things."

Kathy looked annoyed at him, but before anyone could argue the point a sinister laugh echoed through the hallway. They clung to each other for a moment then scattered wildly, racing in all directions, looking for a way out—any way out. Every time one of them opened a door, it slammed shut, locked.

"Find a window, find a window, Ty!" Leonard yelled. "Where's that music room with all the windows?"

"We're trapped!" Kathy shouted. "I told you this was a mistake. We're never getting out of here!"

Chapter Four

"Stop panicking, Kathy!" Tyler ordered. "Of course we'll get out of here. You're scaring Christina."

"Speaking of Christina—look at her," Antonio said.

Christina had her eyes closed, swaying to something none of the others could hear. She followed the sounds to a large set of wooden doors at the end of the hallway and reached for a doorknob.

"No, Christina," Tyler begged, afraid something unspeakable lurked beyond the doors. But it was too late.

Christina's eyes danced as the door opened to a dreamlike scene. A staggeringly blinding light brightened the hallway as the door opened wide allowing everyone to hear what Christina had been hearing: elegant, delightful tones—harmonies of innocence and beauty.

When they stepped into the room, the aroma of blossoms spilled over them even more powerfully than before. Hundreds of colorful exotic plants and flowers swayed before them—some towering twenty feet high, spiraling toward a massive glass dome—bending and moving in exact time to the music.

Their attention was drawn to a gold pedestal in the center of the room. Upon it stood a crystal harp containing an energy field of dancing, swirling light, sending out the music, which filled the bright room. Enchanted, they gathered around it and saw that it lit up a grand, ornately carved entrance to what must be another large room, as though the elegant conservatory led to an even greater chamber beyond.

They stood in silence in the plant-filled room, marveling at the gigantic mahogany doors leading into the next room. Tyler stepped through the archway and threw open the doors revealing the large room with colorful stained glass windows they'd seen from the street.

"This is it, the room where I heard the music last night!" He smiled, pointing to the piano at the far end of the room. The others hurried to join him.

They stared in awe at the room. The storm had passed and the light of the moon shone through the arched windows highlighting the majesty of this chamber and its gallery of unusual musical instruments. No one was prepared for the grandeur that awaited them. The power of the room seemed to momentarily erase the awareness of their bizarre predicament. Richly-grained hardwood floors shined to perfection, reflecting a row of grand pedestals with busts of familiar composers like Bach and Beethoven.

A strange ray of light hit a stained glass window at just the right angle, and cast a prism of light upon the piano and the contents of the room in all the colors of the rainbow—red, orange, yellow, green, blue, indigo and violet.

A tiny spark of light surprised them as it arose from inside the grand piano. All eyes followed the spark as it grew brighter and brighter, much brighter than the rays of the sun, filling the entire parlor. The ever-increasing brightness overtook the shapes of the statues turning them one by one into pillars of light.

"What's happening?" Kathy whispered, as the dazzling

light swirled through the room.

Christina danced into the center of the room. The others joined her in the light, while visions of young people playing instruments flooded every corner.

A mighty gust of wind blew open a window and blasted through the music parlor, wildly blowing the draperies and whipping their hair and clothing. The wind was so strong and the light was so blinding that it became impossible to move or to see anything.

Then, very mysteriously, all was calm and silent. The blazing light disappeared. They stood, awestruck. On the other side of the room behind the grand piano, in another ornately carved archway, a pair of enormous Golden Doors appeared and slowly began to open. It was daytime on the other side.

They looked at each other, wide-eyed, not moving.

Tyler took Christina by the hand when the piano began to play—the same music he had heard the night before. Christina's eyes danced in hope, as if she might see her mother sitting on the piano bench, playing that beloved little tune for her. Her eyes filled with tears as she watched what appeared to be a piano playing itself.

"It's just a player piano," Leonard said.

"No, it isn't." Tyler argued.

At that very moment, there appeared the first traces of a hand moving skillfully over the ivories, then another hand. Before long, arms appeared and then shoulders, first the right then the left.

Everyone stepped away from the piano.

Then a formal jacket appeared and legs took shape, forming a wispy body of the man Tyler had seen the night before. The translucent figure seated at the piano played Mrs. Harrington's special final chords. Kathy was stunned. She'd heard those extra chords many times.

A sense of warmth and wellbeing filled them.

Tyler pointed, "Look!"

The transparent man pushed back the piano bench, stood and turned toward them. Kathy's jaw dropped. Leonard shook his dark head of hair in disbelief.

Tyler, once he recovered from shock, beamed as the image grew clearer and there appeared a cheerful face with a mane of wild silvery hair framed by a high white collar.

Dr. Benjamin Erastus Fuddle

A great teacher will lead you, Tyler recalled his mother's words. He observed that the gentleman's dark blue coat and tails looked rather more jaunty and formal than most scholars would wear.

Once fully materialized, the visitor floated into their midst, landing with ease right in front of Tyler, who stood in rapt attention. He knew he was standing before his long awaited Teacher. The others didn't know what to think of the man or ghost or whatever he was, and looked on in amazement.

He appeared to be an older gentleman, perhaps seventy-five years of age, distinguished and refined in his appearance, but with a slight hint of untidiness. His blue eyes shone with a marvelous kindness. His expression, indeed his whole manner, communicated a sense of purposefulness.

"I am Dr. Benjamin Erastus Fuddle at your service," the man said with a sweeping bow. "Welcome to my music parlor."

His presence calmed their fears; but they could not help but stare.

"Great heavens!" he said in a befuddled manner, looking closely at each of them. He then beamed directly at Tyler. "So pleased to meet you at last, Tyler Harrington!"

"But...but how could you know who I am?"

"I know many things, of which you shall soon be aware," he said, smiling. Christina went up to him and hugged him. He gave her a look that told her he understood exactly who she was and patted her hand.

Leonard could contain himself no longer. "With all due respect, sir, how did you do what we just saw? You..." He was almost at a loss for words. "... you appeared out of thin air. That's impossible!"

Dr. Fuddle studied the expression of doubt on Leonard's face. "Impossible? Why, that's one of my favorite words. When people start claiming impossible, I shout 'inevitable!'"

"But there has to be a way of explaining this whole *illusion*, or whatever it is." Leonard waved his arms at Dr. Fuddle and the Golden Doors, attempting to reach deep within his intellect for an explanation. "What's happened violates the laws of nature. That just *can't* happen, can it?"

"Well, now you see otherwise," Dr. Fuddle said. "Your friend who led you here has believed all along." Tyler smiled and Dr. Fuddle continued. "I'm so pleased you've all followed his lead."

"Now, tell me, as I am most eager to know, my courageous band of adventurers, did you enjoy the historical artifacts of music in my home?"

Their eyes opened wide. Kathy was more embarrassed than she'd ever been in all her thirteen years. "I'm so sorry, sir! I apologize for what we've done. It was very wrong and disrespectful and I was against it all along, I'll have you know."

"I appreciate your sincerity, my fine young lady." Dr. Fuddle looked thoughtfully at all of them. "But you are supposed to be here."

"*Supposed* to be here?" Kathy asked. "This was planned?"

"Indubitably!" Dr. Fuddle announced and smiled, looking proudly at Tyler. "I knew you'd come when you heard that music last night. You've done very well following your intuition and pushing past your fears, young man."

The others studied Dr. Fuddle, finding him both wonderful and bizarre.

"But who *are* you exactly?" Leonard asked.

"I am first and foremost a teacher of music. I've been privileged to teach music and collect exotic musical instruments throughout time. But before I explain why we are all here together, let's get to know one another."

He signaled for Kathy. "Let's begin with you. Tell me about yourself, Kathy."

She took a moment to brush her sleeves, adjust her glasses and fix her purse securely on her arm while she thought. Once she had collected herself, she stood as tall and straight as possible and pronounced, "I'm a music student and quite proud of my six years of piano lessons from Tyler's mother. But I intend to be a fashion designer. And I'm certainly glad I've survived this disaster so far."

Everybody laughed.

"I am, as well, my dear. It's very nice to meet you." Dr. Fuddle shook her hand, releasing soothing warmth to her with his touch. "You have far more courage than you give yourself credit for."

"This is all so unexpected," Kathy said. "Am I properly dressed?"

Dr. Fuddle looked at her perfectly matched clothing ensemble with admiration. "Worry not, my dear. I can see that you have perfect taste. You'll enjoy meeting the Countess, who is up to date on all the latest Parisian and European fashions."

Countess? Kathy had no idea who he was talking about.

"Would you be willing to accept a great challenge for good reason?" Dr. Fuddle asked.

"I'm not sure about that." Then she noticed his quizzical look. "Well, I suppose so. But only for a very good reason."

He nodded his appreciation. "That's important for me to know."

Kathy wondered what he meant, fearing she might regret it.

Dr. Fuddle continued the introductions, turning to Leonard. "I must say, Leonard Lang, that I'm highly intrigued by the award-winning work of your father."

Leonard swelled with pride, and did a double take. "But how did you know about my father?"

"Well, my boy, he is, after all a very famous biochemist, is he not? But I would like to know more about you."

"Much like my father, my passion is scientific inquiry. Therefore, I'm sure you'll understand when I say that all this

33

is most perplexing. I'm more into quantum physics than magic."

"Ah, but you just might discover all 'this' is much closer to your quantum physics than you imagine."

Dr. Fuddle's remark left Leonard speechless.

"With your love of mathematical precision, I'm sure the counterpoint of Bach, where he combines more than one melody, will greatly interest you, Leonard."

"Maybe," Leonard said, "but I'm quite curious to know why you say we're supposed to be here."

Dr. Fuddle nodded, noting his concern. "I promise you, young man, if you'll extend your patience a bit longer, you'll receive a full explanation."

Leonard seemed satisfied for the moment.

Dr. Fuddle addressed Antonio. "And you, my young friend?"

"I've got to tell you, you seem like a pretty cool dude, Dr. Fuddle."

"Don't call him 'dude,'" Kathy scolded. "Where are your manners?"

"It's quite all right, Kathy," Dr. Fuddle said, looking at his spiked black hair, torn blue jeans and V-necked T-shirt. "Antonio has a unique way of expressing himself."

"So you're a music teacher? You know, I like music, too," Antonio said. "I play drums in my friends' band but they want to kick me out."

"Well, why would they want to do that?" Dr. Fuddle asked.

"They say I don't have rhythm, much less talent."

"You say this about Antonio?" Dr. Fuddle asked, looking at the others.

"Not these guys," corrected Antonio. "I'm talking about my other friends."

"Some friends," Tyler muttered.

"I see, Antonio," Dr. Fuddle said. "Well, you look like you have powerful potential, musically and otherwise."

"I'm trying to learn," he said, flashing a dazzling smile. "My dad's a pro ballplayer, you know. Just the minor leagues, but he's good. I'd like to be really good at something."

Dr. Fuddle smiled. "I believe you do and I believe you shall be. But expect the unexpected. I know you're open to that."

"Yeah, man." With a look from Kathy he amended that to "Dr. Fuddle, sir."

Dr. Fuddle directed his attention to Tyler and Christina. A look of satisfaction spread over his face, which managed to be charming and quirky at the same time.

"My sister's name is Christina," Tyler said. "She can't speak."

"Ah, but she speaks clearly in her own way, does she not?" Tyler nodded.

Dr. Fuddle looked very serious for a moment. "That you've learned to trust your instincts at such a young age is a truly wonderful thing, Tyler."

Happy to receive the compliment, he said: "I'm so happy to meet you, Dr. Fuddle. I know our mother opened the way for us to meet. I could feel it in my bones."

"You're exactly right, young man. That feeling prompted you to look through my window." Dr. Fuddle studied Christina. "You've just turned seven years old, haven't you, my child?"

"Yes!" Tyler exclaimed. "How'd you know that?"

"You'll understand in time." He gazed down at their perplexed faces. "I'm grateful to meet all of you and that we're all finally here together. Let me explain what has happened and why you're here."

For a moment grief overcame Dr. Fuddle's joyful expression. The teacher's voice sounded like it came from far away as he began.

"In the beginning," he said, "music created the universe." He paused and allowed the power of this great truth to settle in. "The great scepter of power, the Gold Baton, became known to humans and as time passed, men realized that this treasure had the power to give voice to every living thing, to create harmony and peace throughout the world. No one, not even the greatest scholars know where it came from, but its power was passed down through the ages from mind to mind and from heart to heart, even when it disappeared from the material world. No one alive can fully grasp this mystery."

He paused and motioned toward the Golden Doors. "These doors are a portal into the realm of Orphea, the land of eternal music and beauty. The Prophecy of Orpheus predicted a great time of tribulation would strike Orphea, when chaos would rule."

"They've been predicting that for centuries on earth, too," Leonard said.

"Yes, you are correct," Dr. Fuddle replied.

"Well, at least we don't have to worry about that yet," Antonio said.

Dr. Fuddle looked at him seriously, then at Tyler. "Oh really?" Tyler said, "What about the vandalism at school that we never used to have? And those so-called friends of yours? They never used to act that way!"

"Let's not talk about them, all right?" Antonio looked embarrassed.

"Tyler's right, Antonio. Why do you want to be friends with them?" Kathy asked.

Dr. Fuddle said gently, "Let's get on with our story. But it's not surprising that you are thinking about these things, as you will find out."

"You see, that great source of power, the Gold Baton, disappeared. No one knows how exactly. All we could see was that

36

little by little darkness was taking over the land. The stars were flickering out." He looked at Tyler, whose face showed his astonishment. *So he wasn't imagining things!* "Little by little our beauty was decaying and our music stopped playing. And worst of all, our young people were slowly disappearing. Some have returned, but they have not come back the same as they were. They've been horribly changed, as if by some ghastly spell, and now they've become instruments of chaos." He looked at Tyler again. "It is necessary to get the Gold Baton back before everything in Orphea is destroyed."

Tyler's brow furrowed, "My mother had a disturbing vision about a terrible disaster."

Dr. Fuddle nodded and looked directly into their eyes.

"The prophecy also declared that there would be five Messengers of Music sent from earth to Orphea to reclaim the Gold Baton, to heal the land."

The group was silent as they struggled to grasp the significance of Dr. Fuddle's words. For once in her life, not even Kathy had something to say.

Christina wrote for only Tyler to see, "Mama said something great for you to do?"

Tyler nodded.

Dr. Fuddle looked kind, but unsmiling. "Now Tyler, and the rest of you? This is your choice. You must decide if you'll go forward with me into Orphea to fulfill your destiny or return to life as you knew it. I can tell you that you *are* prepared for this moment. You already have everything within you to succeed. And I will prepare you further and give you the resources that you need."

He paused with a most serious look on his face.

"But I must forewarn you, if you choose to go with me to Orphea, it will be very dangerous."

Chapter Five

Tyler took Christina by the hand. "Dangerous or not, this is what I must do Christina—what Mom wanted me to do. Are you with me?"

The smile on Christina's face left no doubt that she was up to the task. They stepped forward to stand beside Dr. Fuddle.

"Count me in, too," Antonio said, joining them alongside Dr. Fuddle.

"Leonard, make them stop!" Kathy begged. "Who knows what's on the other side of those doors?" She thought about asking Dr. Fuddle to help her get back home, but Leonard cut short her idea.

"I must see this for myself," was all he said and this seemed to be enough to persuade Kathy, who reluctantly joined the others.

Dr. Fuddle led Tyler and Christina through the Golden Doors onto a marble terrace with the others right behind him. As their eyes became accustomed to the fading light, the shock of what lay before them rendered them momentarily mute. It was obvious they were no longer on the grounds of the mansion in their neighborhood.

They gazed with wonder, looking at one another with eyes open wide, transfixed. The diverse scene, alive with flowers and trees and shrubs of every shape and size, was unlike anything they had ever seen. But even more wondrous yet was that everywhere they looked, they not only saw, but *heard* and *felt* their new surroundings. Even though they remained standing exactly where they were, it was if they were virtually transported into a wondrous memory.

"Look around you," Dr. Fuddle said. "Every step of this journey will automatically become a part of you. Everything you see, everything you hear, everything you feel…" his words trailed off and he broke into a radiant smile. "Every aspect and every particle, both seen and unseen, will become a permanent part of you from this moment forward."

As Tyler and Christina gazed upon a grove of sparkling trees found they felt themselves transported onto the stage in the middle of a performance of Tchaikovsky's *Nutcracker* ballet that their mother had taken them to. Christina became Clara and Tyler became Fritz, the children in the ballet. And lo and behold, who should be there with them but Mrs. Harrington, their mother, playing the role of Clara and Fritz's mother. It was so comforting to be in her presence again that neither of them ever wanted to leave the scene.

While Kathy gazed upon tall Italian cypress trees bordering a rolling hillside, in her mind's eye she was transported instantly into the middle of the magnificently costumed opera, Puccini's *Madame Butterfly* that her mother had taken her to.

Antonio couldn't take his eyes off clusters of gigantic broad-leafed trees adorned with red flowers with petals the size of plates. The towering trees reached into the mists of a waterfall that tumbled down the mountain. Suddenly, he envisioned being in the midst of a Brazilian tribe beating their drums in a chorus of blood-stirring rhythms.

39

But Leonard, with no specific musical recollections, stood on the marble terrace unable to believe his eyes. "How could this be?" he asked with childlike innocence.

Dr. Fuddle took his time before answering, looking up into the blue sky with a far-away expression. "Because it was meant to be. Orphea has always been here. You have to know where to find it."

Leonard could hardly allow himself to accept what he was experiencing. He bolted past Kathy, to step back into the music parlor, attempting to discern reality. Then he ran back out toward the others, hoping the entire enchanting scene of Orphea would be gone. Instead, he stared in disbelief. Nothing had changed. "This just can't be!"

"Well, it is," Tyler said, "because here we are."

"Where are we exactly? Where is this Orphea?" Leonard asked.

Kathy thought she saw a twinkle in Dr. Fuddle's eyes as he answered. "It's beyond the canopy of stars."

Tyler followed Dr. Fuddle a few steps farther out onto the terrace, leading Christina by the hand down several steps. The others followed. Lakes decorated with fountains and flowered gardens accented the landscape. In the distance, mountain ranges towered above green meadows and crystal blue lakes.

"Enjoy this beauty, because this is one of the last places in Orphea that isn't at least partially destroyed," Dr. Fuddle said.

Tyler ushered his sister and friends down more white steps onto a shiny marble path lined with flowers and shrubbery. Every one but Leonard was filled with the warmth of their recent musical memories and adventures. Ahead, the path led past the lakes and into the forest.

Christina was the first to notice that the leaves of the trees and shrubs, plants and flowers appeared unlike any seen on earth. She stopped, cupping a leaf in her hand and motioned to Kathy.

"Look at this, everyone," Kathy said.

Tyler, Antonio and Leonard stepped over, peering closely at the unusual leaf.

"And look at *this* one!" Kathy exclaimed.

The leaf itself resembled earthly leaves, but it was covered in musical symbols, some recognizable, but others much more complex. Hundreds, maybe thousands of symbols were visible in every part of the leaf.

Musical sounds arose in the distance as they walked on, accompanied by other faintly familiar sounds, like the sounds of chimes and birds chirping—but not like bird songs they'd ever heard. Then clearly they heard the sound of violins.

Kathy moved closer to Leonard. She looked off into the distance and felt a refreshing rush of air, but stopped. "I don't think we should go any farther."

"Why?" Leonard asked.

"Why?" Kathy responded, bewildered. "Because we may never get back home—that's why!"

"We won't wander far from this path, and we'll always know our way back," Tyler said.

"Yes," Dr. Fuddle said. "I can assure you your way home will always remain on the other side of the Golden Doors."

"Besides, I have to figure out this entire Orphea scene for myself," Leonard said. "If you go back, you'll have to go alone."

Kathy winced but remained by his side.

The sounds of birds, chimes and music stopped all at once.

Two young girls approached along the path holding violins, dressed in daytime clothing of the eighteenth century. Kathy was taken aback by their floor-length dresses with high-waist bodices and lace caps on their curls, tied under their chins.

The girls greeted Dr. Fuddle then turned to the others. "Welcome to Orphea," said the first girl. "We knew that you were on your way. Almost everyone knows by now."

"What?" Antonio said. The five friends looked at each other, questioning.

"You *knew?*" Tyler looked puzzled. The girl was about his age, and he thought she was very beautiful. Her skin shone like deep brown silk, her dark eyes radiated great warmth.

"Yes, everyone here in Orphea has been expecting you. Orphea is where lovers of music dwell after they have sown the seeds of harmony elsewhere. As lovers of music from Earth, you have a special purpose here."

She extended her hand in friendship. "My name is Juliet and this is my friend Elizabeth."

The second girl stepped forward to shake their hands. She was stocky, lacking the elegance and beauty of her friend, but Kathy instantly admired her fiery red hair. "Are you the ones who played that beautiful music?"

"Yes, I'll show you." Elizabeth raised her violin to her chin and played such an intricate fast-paced melody it seemed as though her violin would catch fire. She transformed from her somewhat awkward appearance into a being of confidence, enchanting them with her music. "Our music has always been our magic," she said. "Now it's our protection."

"What do you mean?" Tyler said.

"We'd love to show you more," Juliet said, and turned to Dr. Fuddle for permission.

He smiled and they all followed the girls who led them down the path. Beside a meandering stream under a willow tree stood a gazebo where a string quartet played a slow, touching piece of music. Walking farther along they came to a village surrounded by garden walls covered with flowering vines. Everywhere they looked, young children played instruments together as naturally as laughing or playing games. In fact, these were their games.

Leonard spotted two boys about his age playing dueling cellos. "That looks challenging," he commented.

"Yeah," agreed Tyler with a hint of longing in his voice, remembering how his mother always wanted him to play an instrument.

"We were all happy like this once, but all of that is changing now," Elizabeth said. "Our beautiful existence is collapsing before our eyes. Only the strongest of us have survived this far."

"Many have disappeared from other villages and are not yet found," Juliet said. "And others seem to be part of an evil scheme."

"And no one knows who might be next," Dr. Fuddle added.

"I knew this all looked too good to be true," Kathy said. "We'd better go back for sure."

"Oh, no, please don't," Juliet pleaded. "You'll be glad you didn't."

"We hope..." Elizabeth muttered under her breath.

"You'll *love* the palace and the fashions here!" Juliet said confidently. "Come on." Kathy's eyes lit up for just a moment.

They walked into the center of the village square, where the sight of the normal hustle and bustle of people going in and out of shops quieted their fears. "That's Nannerl's Dress Shop!" Juliet exclaimed.

"Who's Nannerl?" Kathy asked.

"Mozart's sister," Dr. Fuddle replied. "You'll get to meet her directly along with many others."

"And see that over there?" Elizabeth said pointing. "That's Schubert's Sheet Music and More—where we buy all our music."

Christina skipped up to a window filled with dolls of all shapes and sizes wearing exquisite dresses. She looked at them, then looked at Dolly, hugged her and skipped away, satisfied. Tyler smiled.

"This is one of our favorite places!" Elizabeth declared, leading them into a quaint little shop called Bellini's Bakery, named after the Italian composer. "Everything here is named after musicians and composers." The smell of cinnamon and freshly baked bread welcomed them as they stepped into a large colorful showroom with cases of breads and pastries.

Children with their parents dressed in clothing from long ago, sampled delicate artistic-shaped treats, all with strange titles, like Leonin Lemon Delights and Bruckner Brownies. Men in top hats and ladies with frilly bonnets glided from one display to another, chatting with those working behind the counters. One elegant woman said, "We'd like twelve dozen orders of Britten Brittle as soon as possible, please!" But beneath their pleasant faces, there lurked an unmistakable undertone of fear.

They had stopped in front of a large shop whose sign read: "Igor Stravinsky's Instrument Sales and Repair."

"That's the shop that makes most of Orphea's instruments," Dr. Fuddle said.

"We both got our violins there," Juliet announced proudly, holding up her violin.

"And when I dropped my metronome and broke it into hundreds of pieces," Elizabeth added, "they had it put back together before you could count three beats!"

"But now follow me," Dr. Fuddle said, "and you'll see where we store the greatest treasures of Orphea."

Tyler, Christina and their friends felt safe with Dr. Fuddle, Juliet and Elizabeth. Something about their energies filled them with a sense of peace and trust. They had no thoughts of being in danger as long as they were with them. A fleeting fear of being in Orphea without them paralyzed Tyler, but only for the brief instant that he let it enter his mind. After all he'd been through, Tyler had become much better at stopping bad thoughts when they came to him.

"This," Dr. Fuddle said, "is the most fascinating of all places in Orphea." He walked them through a grand doorway, its marquee read: ORPHEA'S MUSEUM OF MUSIC, *An Interactive Experience*. Ornately decorated signs pointed to various attractions. "Walk Where Mozart Walked" and "A Journey through Beethoven's Life and Times": *Line Begins Here*. Beyond the doorway an immense building lined with columns, much like an ancient Greek coliseum, loomed large before their eyes. But something was amiss. Uniformed men stood at attention, "armed" with double basses and cellos. Some even stood watch on the roof.

"They look like guards!" Antonio exclaimed.

"They are," Elizabeth said.

"It was never like this before the Gold Baton disappeared," Juliet said sadly. Tyler and his friends were disturbed by the presence of the guards and could sense looming danger.

"But don't worry, everything is safe here—at least for the time being," Dr. Fuddle said. No one looked convinced. "We must move along. It's time to show you what is happening to Orphea."

Juliet sighed. "Yes, we can't put it off any longer..."

Tyler felt the hair stand up on the back of his neck. *What are we getting into?* he thought. *But since we've come this far we have to keep going.* He and the others slowed their pace, not sure they were ready to face what was next.

Dr. Fuddle and the girls led them farther down the path. The view changed drastically. The forest grew very dense, with trees and weeds pressed against the edges of the polished marble path. Tyler noticed sorrow behind the fragile smile on Dr. Fuddle's face and then observed the reason all around them—decay everywhere, brambles choking out the flowers.

"What's going on? Why is it like this all of a sudden?" Kathy asked.

"Look over there." Antonio pointed to small cottages, which had been covered with graffiti, their windows smashed.

The few young people remaining in the almost deserted village wore faces dark with despair, huddled in the corners shivering. There was no music here, only chaos.

"What's wrong with them?" Tyler asked.

"They're afraid for their lives. Many of their friends were once like us, but were lured into Dis, the part of Orphea that has been corrupted," Juliet explained. "They came back, and damaged everything you see here."

The sky darkened, and everyone became uneasy. A gang of boys caught sight of them and rushed toward Tyler, Christina and their friends, screaming, "Go away! We don't want you here!" Their voices grated, scarcely sounding human. Christina held her hands over her ears while Tyler, Leonard and Antonio tried to shield Christina and Kathy.

Dr. Fuddle reached beneath his coat, producing a large silver lyre from a small pocket. He strummed on the instrument until the music grew louder and louder and other harmonious sounds joined in from afar. The attackers immediately stopped their bullying and ran out of sight, plugging their ears.

"I'm afraid you'll learn quickly that you have enemies here," Dr. Fuddle said. "Enemies that will use any means necessary to stop us from accomplishing what we must do."

Chapter Six

Tyler and his friends stood in shock at Dr. Fuddle's last words.

"Will use any means necessary to stop us?" Kathy echoed.

"Yes," confirmed their guide. He paused to let the meaning sink in, then added, "This will be the greatest challenge of your lives. But you will also reap the greatest rewards when you succeed."

Dr. Fuddle strummed his lyre once more and this time produced a fine carriage with six Hanoverian dappled gray horses. "We must proceed in style to Countess Thun's palace," he said, nodding to Kathy.

"They're magnificent," Tyler said, stroking the mane of the lead horse. He half expected his hand to go right through the horse as if it were a phantom, but it didn't. The horse was real, just as real as everything else they'd seen so far in Orphea. Dr. Fuddle led the five friends into the coach while Juliet and Elizabeth chose to sit in front with the driver. The six of them fit quite comfortably inside on the two plush leather seats facing each other.

The coach proceeded swiftly through the forest, passing

beautiful mountains with peaks of all shapes and sizes. Unusual fragrant scents, like exquisite floral bouquets, drifted over them as they rode through the hills.

Tyler sat across from Leonard and realized that everything Leonard had ever believed was suddenly turned upside down. He smiled across at him. Leonard shrugged, half-smiling back.

The carriage slowed when it came to a clearing with an enormous stone gate with a sign that read:

THE PALACE OF COUNTESS THUN

The carriage turned left onto a tree-lined avenue and stopped at a guard station.

"You may proceed!" the guard shouted, seeing it was Dr. Fuddle and his guests.

The driver slapped the reins of the horses, which trotted onto a majestic cobblestone drive that bordered a glistening lake. Like a mirror the lake reflected the sky and the stately trees on either side of its waters. Far off in the distance stood the most jaw-dropping sight the friends had ever seen—a palace more spectacular than any picture from a book of fairy tales. Huge columns graced the front of the massive ornate palace. Three-story wings stood on either side.

"Here we are," Dr. Fuddle declared.

"Holy Mother!" Antonio gasped. "This is bigger than the Taj Mahal."

The coach came to a halt directly in front of the high rows of steps leading up to the gigantic carved wooden doors. They were excited by the luxury of the palace, and were about to jump out of the carriage to explore its wonders.

"You must wait a moment, my most excellent friends. You have an important decision to make before you go in. All the people of the land are gathered in the banquet hall to welcome you, for you are their heroes. They see you as saviors who have come to rescue them from the total destruction of all they

DR. FUDDLE AND THE GOLD BATON

know and love. They are here to support you in your great task—in our challenge together. But if you ask me to turn the coach around and take you back to the Golden Doors, they will be disappointed yet understanding, for we are asking so much of ones so young. If you choose to step into that palace, it will be much more difficult to turn back once you see the look of hope in their eyes."

The friends looked around at one another, considering Dr. Fuddle's words.

"There is one more thing you need to know. If each one of you succeeds, we all succeed, for together we make up the whole. Each one of you is equally important."

They beamed and sat a little taller.

"If, however, even one of you fails? I tell you this, the mission will fail."

A stricken look passed over Antonio's face.

"That's a lot of responsibility," Leonard said.

Kathy's thoughts whirled around in her head. *It's our duty! But what if I fail? I can't win—I'll be in trouble here and at home. I'll only stay if Leonard stays.*

As for Tyler and Christina, they knew without a doubt that this was their destiny. Their only worry—besides the mortal danger of course—was that their friends might very well say no. And without them, there was no mission.

Dr. Fuddle stepped out of the carriage and closed the door behind him to give them privacy to discuss their decision. He helped Juliet and Elizabeth down from the carriage and ushered them to a smiling guard who led them through a courtyard gate. Dr. Fuddle walked up the first row of steps to wait for a decision from his five friends. Within moments, Tyler opened the doors, leading the others out of the coach and up the steps to approach their mentor.

Antonio, as usual, bounded ahead, but waited for his friend

to speak first. Tyler's steps were as purposeful as ever. He looked directly into Dr. Fuddle's eyes and stated clearly, "I want to press on. No turning back for me. I want to do it for my mother and my sister." Christina smiled and squeezed his hand, knowing he felt proud of himself for leading them into this grand adventure.

Dr. Fuddle smiled and nodded his approval and thought, *Good for you, steadfast lad, and in acting out of the goodness of your heart, you shall discover a deeper meaning for yourself.*

Antonio didn't hesitate one minute. "I don't mind a little danger—It'll be exciting. I'm going in!"

"Outstanding, our brave risk-taker!" Dr. Fuddle said.

Kathy and Leonard walked slowly away from the coach. Kathy, unusual for her controlling nature, felt conflicted. She couldn't imagine what was *really* going on. She looked at the billowing branches of the nearby trees and thought they looked like enormous arms, warning them to turn back. The wind blew leaves off the trees into tiny spirals that collapsed with eerie whispers to the ground. A strange chill hovered in the air.

Leonard made the decision for both of them. His scientific curiosity had gotten the best of him. "Come on, Kathy. Let's go with them and see what happens. This crowd obviously needs to be balanced on the side of logical thinking."

Kathy smiled.

Tyler shook Leonard's hand as he joined the others and Christina hugged Kathy.

"Well, I'm not sure what we've gotten ourselves into, but I must confess I'm interested in the musical possibilities here," Kathy said. "But don't be surprised if I'm even more interested in the fashion." Everyone laughed.

Dr. Fuddle was pleased. "I venture to predict you'll learn much about both music and fashion and surprise yourself. Excellent! Let us proceed."

Tyler reached for Christina's hand and she smiled back affectionately. Everyone followed Dr. Fuddle as he walked up the last tier of marble steps to the giant doors of the palace.

"Tell us exactly, who is Countess Thun?" Kathy asked.

"She is the hostess of this land." Dr. Fuddle smiled. "The Countess continues doing here what she did when she passed through her life on Earth: welcoming guests, feeding them delectable food, and arranging for the most wonderful music to be played. She was Mozart's favorite hostess."

"You're not going to tell me Mozart's here, too, are you?" Kathy asked.

"Most certainly! All the composers and music lovers are here," Dr. Fuddle said proudly, "unless they're busy sowing musical seeds elsewhere."

Kathy looked at Tyler stunned. Tyler wondered what Dr. Fuddle meant by the last part, and wondered if it had anything to do with his mother. *Surely our mother would've greeted Christina and me if she were in Orphea*, he thought to himself.

Dr. Fuddle reached for a huge brass door knocker shaped like a lion's face.

"Enter ye," the door knocker said before Dr. Fuddle even had a chance to clang it against the door. They all smiled.

The doors slowly opened.

Chapter Seven

"Please go in," Dr. Fuddle said. They stepped into a grand, oval-shaped hall of the richest sky-blue color imaginable.

Tyler poked Antonio. "Did you see Leonard examining the door knocker?"

"Yeah," Antonio replied, "he's still looking for hook-ups to electronic sound equipment." They both grinned.

A serious-looking man scurried toward Dr. Fuddle.

"I'm afraid Countess Thun is nowhere to be found!" He wrung his hands nervously.

Tyler felt a sinking feeling at the news.

"She can't be too far away," Dr. Fuddle said, "Everyone follow me and we'll find her."

"How? This place is gigantic!" Kathy exclaimed.

"I have an idea where she might be." They followed Dr. Fuddle through the broad hallways, along a corridor of lavish floor to ceiling mirrors and sure enough, there was Countess Thun, standing alone, staring out a window. Dr. Fuddle walked toward her.

"There you are," Dr. Fuddle said.

As she turned around, it was impossible not to notice the look of dread on her face. She was a small, elegant woman wearing a graceful yellow dress with a blue sash waistband and a tiara bejeweled with precious stones.

"What is it, Countess?" he asked. "Have you seen more of them?"

"Yes, Dr. Fuddle." Her voice was shaky. "I saw a number of the Seiren creatures flying off in the distance. It looked like they were leaving the Lowlands," she said, unable to hide the look of fear on her face. Tyler and the others looked at each other, wide-eyed.

"Were there many of them?" Dr. Fuddle asked, unable to hide his concern.

"Yes, and I'm afraid to report there are more of them than ever."

Kathy clung to Leonard.

"It was hard to tell how many at such a distance," Countess Thun replied. "I could see dozens of them, maybe hundreds, until they disappeared beyond the hills." Her pretty face looked drawn and sad. "And I'm afraid many more of our young people are gone—no doubt under their spell. I don't know how or why they follow them."

"My dear Countess, I must request that you refrain from worrying," Dr. Fuddle said gently. "I am now here to help, as are the Messengers of Music—just as the Prophecy of Orpheus had written."

"As you say, Dr. Fuddle," she replied, instantly changing her expression to a happier one. "I trust the grand design— that all will turn out the way we've prayed. I hope the power of our Art is far greater than this difficulty."

"So, come, and meet our visitors," Dr. Fuddle said.

She turned to them. "Greetings and welcome, my darlings!"

Dr. Fuddle introduced each of them to her by name, but she seemed especially curious about Christina.

"What a precious little doll you have there, Christina! May I see her?"

Christina smiled brightly and offered Dolly to the Countess.

"Oh, my. Wherever did you find such a jewel?" she asked, enchanted. "I love her porcelain face and her elegant floral frock with the pinafore."

"I gave the doll to her when our mother passed away," Tyler explained. "And I don't think she's ever let go of her since."

The Countess smiled tenderly, noticing the pull string on the back of the doll. She pulled it and the doll said brightly, "Hello, My name is Dolly!" The Countess said, "How clever," and handed it back to Christina. "Let's proceed to the banquet hall. Please follow me."

"What were the Countess and Dr. Fuddle talking about?" whispered Kathy to Leonard. "There were dozens of what?"

"I don't know," he answered. "It sounded like she said Seirens. We may be getting in over our heads." Kathy cringed and could feel they were in danger.

The Countess led them down the hall, past statues, paintings, and dozens of fragrant floral arrangements. She noticed Christina lingering at one of the arrangements, observing what the others had missed—wilted flowers struggling to survive in the fresh bouquets. She kissed the top of Christina's head then ushered everyone up to two tall doors with spectacular carvings on either side.

Dr. Fuddle opened the doors to the sight of hundreds of people seated at countless round tables. Kathy gasped when she saw that all the ladies and girls wore the highly detailed hooped gowns of the eighteenth century.

"What's the *deal* with all these people dressed like this?" Antonio snickered.

"Obviously it's court fashion from previous times," Kathy said.

"You're absolutely right, my dear," the Countess said to Kathy. "We women came into our power with The Enlightenment, the movement that raised our culture to new heights. For the first time in centuries, we could compete with men because knowledge and the Arts were most important and we often topped men in both. Just look at how grand everyone appears with their bustles and tall powdered wigs. Musicians from every era are here, but the fashions you see are reserved for such special occasions as this."

"But the men look almost feminine, too, with their wigs and ruffles," Leonard said with disapproval.

"I am so out of place," Kathy moaned, looking down at her layered fall outfit.

"They will love to see what girls on earth are wearing these days, so don't you fret," Countess Thun assured her.

In fact, at that very moment, a wigged fellow and girl about their age approached and greeted them, looking at Antonio's jeans and T-shirt and making a fuss over Kathy's stylish patent leather boots. "Most unusual," the lad commented. The girl said to Kathy, "Those boots are outrageously daring! I do wish I had a pair."

"What did I tell you, darling?" the Countess said. Kathy beamed. Leonard smiled and shook his head.

The crowd chatted in excited tones while an orchestra played softly in the background.

"Our places are reserved up there," Dr. Fuddle said, pointing to a long banquet table on a large stage. "Shall we find our seats?" He led them through the crowd toward the stage, while the Orphean girls swooned at Antonio's good looks.

"This is amazing," Kathy said.

"I'm sure not complaining," Antonio smiled, waving to several beautiful girls in colorful gowns.

Once on the stage, a sudden blast of trumpets pierced the air. The fanfare continued until six singers, three females and three males, strolled onto the stage to perform a rousing song of welcome to all of them. They sang with such gusto they rattled the goblets.

Dr. Fuddle seated Tyler and the others while the singers left the stage. He then stepped to a podium to face the audience. A great hush settled upon the throng.

"I greet you, people of Orphea, in the name of music. As you know, we are now at the most important crossroads in our history as a people devoted to art, and devoted to that force we cherish—music. We must confront an enemy together, but do not be fearful, my friends, for I am here to tell you the good news. You now are no longer alone, for, as the Prophecy of Orpheus has foretold, the Messengers of Music have come to deliver our land from this great hardship."

All eyes turned to Tyler, Christina and their friends and one by one the people seated below rose from their seats. A gradual applause spread throughout the room. Dr. Fuddle motioned for the Messengers to stand.

They humbly bowed, amazed at this unexpected turn of events and gradually assumed a degree of confidence.

Leonard whispered to Kathy before the applause died out. "I didn't realize it would be like this."

"And I'm afraid our parents will be worried. Though I must confess I'm enjoying this admiration." Kathy said. "And oh, look—isn't that Johann Sebastian Bach? And Wolfgang Amadeus Mozart? I wonder who the others are."

Dr. Fuddle waited a moment before continuing. He brought a small scroll out of his pocket, opened it, and read:

When the Hunter of the Unknown shall appear
An act of great courage erases all fear.
Love and strength will unite
Doubt banished by Light
And the Voice of Silence will speak
To those who inwardly seek.

Tyler knew the prophecy was about what the Messengers of Music must do—surely the very act his mother had foretold—that he hoped also meant giving Christina back her voice. He looked at the faces of Leonard and Kathy and wondered if they would stick it out to the end. He also wondered if he himself had the strength to do whatever required great courage.

Chapter Eight

After reading from the prophecy, Dr. Fuddle allowed silence to linger for several moments. He looked into the vast sea of faces, feeling compassion as he viewed the mixture of hope and despair in the eyes of the Orpheans. They appeared to be a people torn by war—struggling to maintain their peaceful traditions—but ravaged by the drastic challenges they faced.

Dr. Fuddle determined to show confidence, to inspire their hope. "And now joining me in the next all-important part of our ceremony—please welcome our beloved composer and friend, Wolfgang Amadeus Mozart." A tremendous round of applause greeted Mozart as he rose from his table. He was a small, but powerful looking man. Seated next to him was his sister Nannerl, pretty, but in a pinched sort of way. She wore a velvety brown dress, and her head was crowned by a mammoth, box-shaped wig.

"Look at that hair!" Antonio whispered to Tyler, not yet grasping the seriousness of the situation.

Mozart took his place behind the podium. "Honored citizens of Orphea, I'm privileged to be here this evening to tell you, do not believe the rumors that we are nearing the end of our great history."

He smiled, nodding to Dr. Fuddle.

"Now, I must admit when I learned about the disappearance of the Gold Baton, our legendary scepter of harmony, I hardly knew what to say or do. The tragic loss of our children, along with the damage to our natural and musical beauty, is almost too much to bear. But hear this—victory must be ours once and for all."

The crowd cheered at the thought of triumph.

"And to remind ourselves of what we are fighting for," continued Mozart, "our remaining talented young musicians have prepared a short piece in honor of our Messengers of Music— my very own, *Eine Kleine Nachtmusik!*"

"What's that supposed to mean?" Antonio asked.

"It means *A Little Night Music*," Kathy said. "My grandparents speak German."

The young people in the orchestra pit stood and bowed to Tyler and his friends. They clapped their bows on their instruments in "applause," as is the tradition among musicians. And then a young man no more than sixteen stepped forward to conduct the piece. The music echoed throughout the banquet hall, bringing smiles to everyone's faces.

"I have to admit, I wish I could play like that," Antonio whispered.

"They're so young!" Kathy said.

"And accomplished," Leonard added.

An unfamiliar feeling stirred in Tyler's heart, surprising him—that of an unknown love and yearning for music. He quickly brushed away a tear, thinking about his mother's music, hoping nobody had noticed. But Dr. Fuddle had seen the tear and smiled to himself.

The musicians played the last few notes with a flourish and

Tyler and his friends led the audience in standing applause.

Mozart beamed and spoke loud enough for all to hear, "We have a very clear strategy. There's no need to worry, my young friends, for you are indeed the long-awaited Messengers of Music, sent to us to deliver our land from darkness and destruction. We must work together to redeem our children and reclaim the Gold Baton."

Dr. Fuddle stepped toward his puzzled looking students and smiled. "We pray that victory will be ours. For it states in the prophecy:

> *And the Messengers of Music will possess*
> *Instruments matched to their prowess*
> *Harnessing magic so powerfully contained*
> *That none of their enemies shall sustain.*

He looked into the eyes of each Messenger. "We'll need for all of you to reach deep within yourselves. You must find the love and strength that resides in your hearts and combine it with thorough training and knowledge." He then opened his arms wide to the people of Orphea. "Let all of us in this great land do everything we can to support our young Messengers."

The audience cheered and when silence returned, Dr. Fuddle motioned for another man to step forward. "And now please help me welcome Johann Albrechtsberger, ladies and gentlemen, the head of the Conservatory, music professor extraordinaire!"

A scientific-looking man carrying a large black case walked from the back of the stage accompanied by two guards armed with cellos.

He nodded in appreciation, handing the case to Mozart.

"Thank you, Professor," Mozart said, opening the case. He then pulled out the strangest-looking device anyone had ever seen. It was a round object about the size of a cake tin with a sparkly blue metal finish. Two shiny metal rods projected from its center holding special lenses and mirrors. He pushed a button to turn it on and a bright blue light shone onto the wall. Several people in the audience gasped.

"This," Dr. Fuddle said, holding up the curious piece of equipment, "is one of the greatest devices our esteemed professors at the Albrechtsberger Conservatory have ever created. It has taken many people to perfect its accuracy. What we have here," he continued with a flourish, "is the ultra-sensitive, ultra-cymatic, ultra-harmonious, Harmonomometer."

Leonard suddenly looked curious for the first time. "The device looks very hi-tech, but what does it do?" he asked.

With obvious pride Dr. Fuddle explained, "With the creation of the Harmonomometer, the once-invisible realm of sound is at last revealed! Your voice is a holographic representation of all that you are and contains all aspects of your energetic field. Now, thanks to this first-of-its-kind instrument, your unique harmonic voice pattern can be seen. We will use it to match you with instruments created by Orphea's greatest craftsmen, according to the sacred instructions of Orpheus."

"Wow," Antonio said loudly.

"Upon hearing your reading, Herr Mozart will assign you the instrument that matches your harmonic voice pattern. We've asked the children of Johann Sebastian Bach to do the honors of presenting each instrument," Dr. Fuddle continued. "And now I will ask each of you to come forward when you hear your name. We will start with the oldest."

"Leonard Lang, please come forward."

Leonard strode toward center stage. Dr. Fuddle placed the glowing Harmonomometer on his conductor's stand and invited Leonard to sing an 'A' vowel sound into its microphone. Suddenly the blue light on the wall was replaced by a beautiful pattern that seemed to be alive as it shimmered and wobbled. Dr. Fuddle looked very pleased, "I see we have a pattern with twelve nodes, a sacred number from ancient times that is very favorable because it symbolizes the twelve notes of the chromatic scale," Dr. Fuddle said.

"The chromatic twelve?" shouted a man at a far away table. "Astounding!"

"So what does the reading mean?" Leonard asked.

"The reading represents a musical masterpiece," Dr. Fuddle replied. "In this case, one of the most intellectual of all compositions entitled *The Art of the Fugue*."

"So how exactly does that apply to me?" Leonard asked skeptically.

Leonard Lang

"The Harmonomometer has shown us that you have a great intellectual capacity and we have therefore matched you precisely to one of the four instruments."

Leonard had remained unconvinced, wondering, *how can we be the supposed Messengers of Music?* He glanced at Kathy and the others, wondering if they were impressed with the Harmonomometer. He didn't know what to think, nothing made sense here.

"Yes," Mozart added. "With the reading verified, you Leonard, receive the cello. And to present you with this instrument, I introduce you to Bach's oldest son, Johann Christoph."

A stately young man came forward, handing Leonard the cello made of varnished pine.

"This magnificent instrument compliments your love for precision," Dr. Fuddle explained. "If you apply yourself, you'll master the skills that will allow your cello to overpower the enemy."

The moment Leonard accepted the instrument, a spark ignited from the cello and shot into his hands. "What just happened? Is this plugged into something?"

"No, Leonard," Dr. Fuddle assured. "That spark means that your cello connected with you because you share the same harmonic vibration. It also means your instrument is protected by a powerful spell. The only way this cello can leave you is for you to pass it on to someone else of your own free will."

Leonard returned to his seat, confused and lost in his thoughts.

"Next," Dr. Fuddle said, "Will Kathy Goldman please come forward?"

Raising her eyebrows at Leonard, she adjusted her glasses and walked center stage, trying not to show how much she loved being the center of attention.

Dr. Fuddle then asked Kathy to make an 'E' vowel sound.

Again a beautiful pattern appeared on the wall, this time with a seven-sided figure, a number that Dr Fuddle said was associated with the seven virtues: Faith, Hope, Charity, Fortitude, Justice, Prudence, and Temperance. Mozart and Professor Albrechtsberger looked very pleased.

"Your reading represents the first of Bach's three works for viola and harpsichord," Professor Albrechtsberger said. Kathy smiled at Leonard, but he remained stone-faced. "Your harmonic voice pattern symbolizes the seven notes of the diatonic scale and your love of beauty and design."

"Which means you receive the viola," Mozart said. A girl named Johanna Bach, who appeared about Kathy's age, came forward with the instrument, handing it to Kathy. "Learning the viola will help you understand the structure and design of music."

Kathy reached for it eagerly. The surge of electrical energy made her hands tingle. "Thank you," she said. She studied the fine craftsmanship of the viola, showing it to her friends.

"That viola has unique timbres or tones, matching your vibrational energy, Kathy," Dr. Fuddle explained. "And now Antonio Romero, please come forward."

Antonio's spiked hair and overall appearance stunned the audience, especially the younger girls. He walked with confidence like he owned the palace. Tyler believed in his friend, and hoped he would soon understand the weight of their purpose in Orphea.

"Can I get a closer look at that thing?" he said to Dr. Fuddle, pointing to the Harmonomometer.

"Of course you may."

Antonio looked it over, peering intently at the strange-looking gadget.

"Okay. I guess I'm ready as I'll ever be," he said.

Dr. Fuddle asked Antonio to make the vowel 'I' into the microphone. At first nothing happened but then slowly, with increasing speed, a beautiful three-sided harmonic voice pattern appeared on the wall.

Dr. Fuddle studied the pattern closely. "Hmmm. Very interesting," he said.

"How come?" Antonio asked.

Dr. Fuddle looked at Mozart. "I'm not surprised, Herr Mozart. This young man has quite the potential."

"Did I break that thing? What'd I do?" Antonio asked.

"No, quite the contrary, Antonio," Dr. Fuddle replied. "You're reading is very unusual."

"But what does the three-sided pattern mean?" Antonio said, flashing a broad smile. Several pretty girls giggled.

"It symbolizes the triplet in drum music and stands for a well known work by a composer named Sergei Prokofiev, the Symphonic Suite entitled *Lieutenant Kijé*, which features the snare drum. Therefore you are assigned the snare drum, matching your desires and your energy," Mozart said. "Johann Christian Bach, please come forward with the drum."

A young man brought the drum to Antonio and when he touched it, the spark was brighter and louder than with Kathy or Leonard. He jumped back to the amusement of the audience.

"This also means you have great inner control, perhaps yet to be discovered," Dr. Fuddle said. "You will surprise yourself at the greatest moment of need."

"Sounds good to me," Antonio said. He returned to his seat with the drum and drumsticks in hand.

Christina's ears perked up when she heard a disturbing noise, like a motor, or a dull roar in the distance. She glanced at Tyler. He hadn't heard it. Then she saw Dr. Fuddle turn his head sharply toward Mozart and the Professor. Several people in the audience shifted uncomfortably in their seats.

"Tyler Harrington, please come forward," Dr. Fuddle said, as if nothing had happened.

Christina wondered if maybe she imagined it.

Tyler noticed Christina's face, sensing she'd heard something the others hadn't. She often heard things other people didn't.

Dr. Fuddle invited Tyler to make an 'O' sound into the microphone, like the 'O' sound of the Harmonomometer. As he did so a beautiful sounding chord emerged from the device, as if Tyler had found a secret key to perfection. A flawless five-sided pattern shimmered on the wall.

Dr. Fuddle looked amazed, "This young man's harmonic voice pattern is a pentagon and symbolizes the interval of the perfect fifth. It contains the sacred mathematical golden ratio, an indicator of great purity!"

"Finally!" Mozart said with a look of triumph.

Tyler looked confused.

"The perfect pentagon stands for Wolfgang Amadeus Mozart!" Dr. Fuddle declared. "And is specifically associated with the first of his *Horn Concertos*."

"And so you, Tyler," Mozart continued, "receive the French horn, which symbolizes perfection, purity and power."

A very young girl named Regina Bach presented the French horn to Tyler.

When Tyler's hand touched the horn, the spark lingered in the air and he felt an electrical current running through his entire body.

By the time he returned to his seat everyone was silent and listening to the noise that Christina had heard earlier.

"And now for our last reading…" said Dr. Fuddle, trying to maintain order in spite of the increasing volume of the distracting noise. He produced the small pocket from beneath his coat and pulled out his lyre, strumming it three times. All at once several dozen guards armed with cellos approached from the back hallways.

"What's going on?" Tyler asked.

"Ladies and gentlemen, we have the situation well under

control," Dr. Fuddle said. "I must ask the guards to take their positions around the grounds and we will continue the presentations."

Quickly the guards left the banquet hall and within seconds the noise stopped entirely. Most of the guests around the tables looked relieved, although others appeared doubtful.

"Now there's one more person," Dr. Fuddle said. "Christina Harrington, please come forward. And Tyler, I invite you to join her, please."

They walked together to the center of the stage and stood side-by-side, holding hands. Dr. Fuddle looked Tyler in the eye. "When you hold someone's hand you connect with them at a deep energetic level," Dr. Fuddle said very seriously. "So by holding your sister's hand her energy will move through you. I ask you now to make an 'U' vowel sound while thinking of Christina. The pattern that forms will be her undeveloped voice energy."

Tyler leaned forward over the Harmonomometer, holding tightly to Christina's hand. He closed his eyes, pictured Christina in his mind's eye, and made a long, slow, 'U' sound into the microphone. Everyone in the audience held their breath. A tiny spot of light emerged and out if it grew a beautiful spiral pattern like a giant sunflower that filled the whole wall. Everyone applauded and people cheered and shouted their congratulations, "Awesome! Amazing! Astounding!"

"Ladies and gentlemen," Dr. Fuddle said, "Let there be no doubt in Orphea from this moment forward, that the ancient revelation has come to pass. This young lady's harmonic voice pattern has created the legendary Fibonacci spiral that contains a series of numbers based on the natural harmonics of all music!"

Dr. Fuddle smiled at Christina and bowed slightly to her. "Christina, that pattern represents the *Ninth Symphony* of

Ludwig van Beethoven, one of the greatest mysteries of all music and the first symphony to use the most perfect of all instruments: *the human voice*."

Christina felt chills throughout her body.

"You, Christina Harrington, must watch and listen carefully while you are here in Orphea and stay close to your brother. What you will receive here remains a mystery to everyone," Dr. Fuddle said, "but we know that the prophecy must be fulfilled, 'the voice of silence will speak.'"

Dr. Fuddle looked tenderly at the five Messengers of Music. "The sacred instruments will not do your work magically. The magic resides within you. The power will come only if you succeed in doing your part—practicing everything we will teach you, and finding your own unique musical gifts. It will take the success of all of you combined to produce victory, for together you make up the whole. Remember, if even one of you fails, the entire mission will fail."

Dr. Fuddle could tell Tyler and Christina were ready for whatever was ahead. As for the others, he sensed they felt enthused for the first time.

"You've now been entrusted with the safe-keeping of your instruments." Dr. Fuddle paused. "Our enemy will use every trick you can imagine to try to take these instruments, so you must always be on guard."

"But now let's celebrate!" Mozart said cheerfully. "We have a very special meal for you this evening, prepared by Chef Joseph, the greatest chef in Orphea."

Chef Joseph, a cheerful looking man with a boyish face came through the kitchen door with his helpers bringing them platters of food of all sorts. There were pleasing scents of delights yet to come, drifting from the kitchen.

"Please enjoy your meal," Mozart said. "And for your entertainment, our court orchestra will play concertos by the great Antonio Vivaldi." Mozart motioned for a man with fiery red hair, who stood briefly and bowed.

Dr. Fuddle led the Messengers back to their seats.

"Our main course today is Dussek Duck," Countess Thun announced, "garnished with la Pouplinière Potatoes and Marinated Mahler Mushrooms. And make sure you eat plenty of the Bellini Bread and Rossini Rolls."

Dr. Fuddle smiled. "You see we derive pleasure out of naming our food in honor of composers, musicians or musical patrons."

While everyone feasted on the delightful food, Christina looked around at the expressions of the people in the banquet hall. Although most people smiled, underneath lurked a brooding mood of doubt.

After the main course there were desserts of all kinds, including Leonin's Lemon Delights, Couperin Cupcakes and a rich, chocolaty Puccini Pudding.

At the end of the banquet the Orpheans shook the Messengers of Music's hands and wished them well. Juliet and Elizabeth even wished Christina's Dolly good luck.

A tempting birdsong in the courtyard gardens drew Juliet and Elizabeth outside to look for the birds among the large tree branches. "Come with us!" Elizabeth called to Kathy.

When Kathy and the others joined them in the courtyard, they witnessed a sight that made their blood run cold. The songs were coming from beautiful birds—but before their eyes the birds shape-shifted into hideous creatures: winged, sharp-toothed, angry, catlike monsters.

"NOOOOOO!" Kathy screamed at the top of her lungs, while the creatures lunged for Juliet and Elizabeth, clutching them with their long claws.

Antonio sprang into action, trying to fight off one of the creatures, while Tyler grabbed at the other. But their efforts were no match for the monstrous sharp claws and powerful bat-like wings. It was too late—the creatures were lifting Juliet and Elizabeth up into the air to carry them away.

Kathy ran inside and screamed to Dr. Fuddle. "They've taken Juliet and Elizabeth!"

Dr. Fuddle and dozens of Orpheans rushed outside.

"We'll get them back," Tyler said, hugging Kathy, shocked at his own heroism.

"You've been hurt!" she exclaimed, examining his bleeding arm. "You were so brave."

"It's nothing," Tyler said, but he didn't mind at all being called brave. What worried him was seeing Leonard's scowling face.

Dr. Fuddle looked deeply saddened. "We'll get every last child of Orphea back into the fold," he said. "Tomorrow we will begin to teach you how to use the power of your instruments and learn the strategies for victory."

The five huddled together with Dr. Fuddle, viewing the silhouettes of Juliet and Elizabeth against a bright full moon being flown far, far away.

Chapter Nine

Darkness drastically changes things—especially in the unfamiliar, lavish world of Countess Thun's grand palace, which no longer felt safe from danger.

The gloom that had settled over Orphea at the end of the banquet filled every inch of Tyler's body. He knew he wasn't the only one of the Messengers of Music who felt the fear that seeped into his bones. As Dr. Fuddle and the Countess led them silently through the dim halls of the palace to a distant wing, words from out of the blue sprang into his mind, *Don't be afraid, Tyler dear. Don't be afraid.* Even though he had no idea where they'd come from, the words comforted him a little.

"Don't be afraid, Christina," he said, squeezing her hand. She barely squeezed back; her mind was full of fear.

The caretakers had long since snuffed most of the candles and chandeliers. As beautiful and plush as the palace seemed, suddenly Tyler was more nervous than he had ever been in his life, in spite of the words he'd just heard in his mind about not being afraid. Every shadow seemed to make the palace appear stranger and more threatening.

Kathy stayed close to Leonard during the long walk to the

visitors' wing and had remained quiet since the capture of Juliet and Elizabeth.

"We must find a way to talk privately," Leonard whispered to Kathy, deliberately lagging behind so the others couldn't hear. She nodded.

Dr. Fuddle, too, seemed quiet. "You will need a good night's rest," he said when they finally reached an oval landing at the foot of a grand stairwell. A dimly-lit chandelier hovered in the darkness far above. "The most important thing now is sleep." He knew his words bore no comfort for the worried Messengers.

Countess Thun led them up a red-carpeted staircase to a suite of two adjoining rooms. "The young men will be in this room," she said pointing to one door, "and the young ladies in that room. Dr. Fuddle has his own private quarters. Good night. Rest well and know you are safe here. May you have pleasant dreams."

The Countess opened the doors to the rooms revealing canopy beds with night clothes laid out on each bed. In the girls' room, two beds fit for princesses were reserved for Christina and Kathy. The boys' room had three single beds. She walked back downstairs. "Good night, Benjamin," the Countess said and walked away to her room while Dr. Fuddle headed for his private suite.

Kathy and Leonard had waited outside their doors. When Leonard was sure the coast was clear, he signaled to Kathy to join him in the room with open doors at the end of the hall-way when everyone is asleep. He whispered, "bring your instrument." They both entered their rooms, closing the doors behind them.

After Kathy felt certain Christina was sound asleep, she tucked the blanket around her, kissed her on the forehead, and quietly slid out of the room with her viola case under her arm.

She waited nervously for Leonard just outside his door.

Leonard crept from his room with his cello and quietly closed the door. Tyler was asleep beneath his bedcovers and Antonio was out like a light.

"What have we gotten ourselves into?" she whispered, walking down the hall.

"I don't know. And how this is happening, I'm not sure," he said. "But I'm thinking we're in some type of wormhole. That piano in Dr. Fuddle's music parlor must somehow have created a time warp. It's possible, or else we wouldn't be here."

Kathy looked scared. "Did you see all those guards at the banquet, Leonard?" she asked, her voice trembling. "There must be a lot more of those awful creatures that took Juliet and Elizabeth!"

"Yes," he replied, "The Countess said she saw dozens, maybe hundreds of them. Those creatures we saw must have been the Seirens."

"How will poor Elizabeth and Juliet ever be found?"

"Well," he said trying to express confidence he didn't feel, "we've got some of the world's most brilliant and creative minds at work with us."

Kathy didn't appear comforted in the least.

"Look, Kathy, I know how much you want to get out of here. I do, too. But we did make a promise when we went into that banquet hall. And you must admit there is an exciting challenge here."

"Well, maybe," Kathy said. She was glad Leonard liked to keep his promises. She even admired his curiosity. He squeezed her arm gently.

They reached the two open doors leading to an ornate sitting parlor. Leonard motioned for Kathy to go in. He closed the doors behind them and they walked to a sofa at the far end of the room to sit down.

"Let's examine these instruments," he said. "It's simply not possible we could master them without years of practice."

"But Mozart said they have special powers."

"You know better than to take anything for granted. Besides, Dr. Fuddle said the magic was within us."

Kathy started to argue, but opened her viola case instead.

"Try it and you'll see you can't even begin to play it. I dare you. You'll see they're not special after all," Leonard challenged.

Kathy Goldman

Kathy lifted the viola and propped it under her chin the way she'd seen professional musicians perform. She raised the bow and pulled it across the strings. The scratchy sounds lingered before fading into the damp air.

"I told you!" Leonard jeered. "It's not a special instrument at all. I know mine won't play for me either."

"Well, maybe it isn't working because I don't believe the magic is in me. Try yours."

Just before Leonard unlatched his case, the doors opened. Kathy gasped, grabbing Leonard's arm.

Much to their surprise, two of Bach's children, Johann Christoph and Johanna entered the room, holding stringed instruments in their hands.

Kathy knew instantly something was wrong. "What are they doing in here?" she whispered.

"I have no idea. I thought all the Orpheans had left for home hours ago," Leonard replied.

Johann Christoph glared at Kathy. "My sister is very sad." His voice was gruff and odd, echoing in the large room.

As they approached, Leonard noticed a strange chill in the air. He stood. Kathy followed his lead.

"Please forgive us," Johanna said, "and don't judge us rude."

Kathy shot Leonard a confused glance as they drew closer. Johanna pointed to their instruments.

"You see," Johann said coldly, "Our father promised those instruments to us. Johanna is horribly upset that he's broken his promise and given them to you."

"Broken his promise?" Kathy asked, surprised.

Leonard looked puzzled.

"Yes," Johanna continued. "I've wanted that viola since I was a little girl. Father always told me it would be mine, but now you have it."

"I'm so sorry," Kathy said. She had no idea how to react to this news. The situation grew more awkward by the second.

"Father promised us these instruments long ago—Mozart lied about them." Johann Christoph said. "Everyone knows about the Prophesy of Orpheus and the sacred instruments. And Father *vowed* I'd have that cello!" Anger flared in his eyes as he pointed to the cello in Leonard's hands. Suddenly his voice softened. He raised his own cello and pointed to his sister's viola. "Swap our instruments with yours. They're just the same, except these instruments will allow you to learn easily. No one will know the difference."

"But we're told we need the special power of these instruments. Dr. Fuddle clearly told us they were to stay in our safe-keeping," Kathy said.

Johann scoffed. "The power of those instruments won't mean a thing to you—you'll never be able to use them. They're too difficult to play. But they'd be very special to us because we're already skilled performers. They're famous instruments and we deserve them. Not you."

Leonard felt insulted and threatened.

"We'll be happy to trade instruments with you," he said, attempting to keep his cool. "But where is your father? Let's discuss this with him privately."

"Yes, we would never want you to be upset," Kathy added.

The smoldering in Johann Christoph's eyes sent chills down Kathy's spine. "Father must not know about this."

Leonard looked at Kathy before he spoke. "May I see your cello first?" he said.

"Yes," Johann said, handing it to Leonard. "Just try this cello and you'll see how easy it is to play. It'll seem like magic."

Leonard took hold of the cello and to his amazement, he created sounds perfectly in tune.

"You see!" Johanna sneered, turning to Kathy. "Now you try this viola."

Kathy tried to remain polite. "This doesn't seem right," she said to Johanna.

"It's more than right, Kathy. It's the way it's supposed to be. I assure you."

The look in Johanna's eyes made Kathy want nothing more than to grab Leonard and run out of the room as fast as they could. Instead she took Johanna's viola and matched Leonard's beautiful tones on her first try.

"Now, if you still don't believe us, try to play as perfectly on the sacred instruments," Johann Christoph said.

Before Kathy admitted she'd already tested the sacred viola unsuccessfully, Leonard picked up his cello and failed to create a single musical sound.

Johann Christoph smirked at Leonard's failed efforts. "So now do you believe us?"

Johanna's eyes glistened like a snake's. "And I have something very special for you Kathy, if you'll just let us have your instruments in exchange for ours." She reached into her pocket and produced a bracelet sparkling with every color of jewel in the rainbow.

"This was my grandmother's," she said tenderly. "I want you to have it to remember me, *Kathy*."

The way she emphasized her name made Kathy feel sick. "I don't know about this," she said.

"Here. Take a look. It's very valuable."

The second Kathy felt the bracelet slip into her palm she knew she had to have it. It was gorgeous. She'd never seen anything like it. It was even more beautiful than any piece of jewelry her mother owned.

"My, this *is* special," Kathy said, dazzled by the sparkling colors.

Leonard could see how much she wanted the bracelet.

"I don't know why we shouldn't make this exchange," he whispered to her, ignoring his own instincts.

"Well, I guess there's no harm done. What could be so special about our instruments anyway?" Kathy added, still spellbound by the glittering gold and gems.

"That's right, Leonard," Johann said. "This swap won't make any difference except your jobs here will be much easier."

Kathy handed her viola over to Johanna and watched Leonard hand over the cello. Within seconds, the exchange was made and Kathy slipped the jeweled bracelet quietly into her purse.

"You won't regret this," Johanna promised. The look in her eyes made Kathy feel faint.

As soon as Kathy and Leonard had left the sitting parlor and were walking down the hallway, Johanna and Johann Christoph burst into fiendish laughter. "That was just *too* easy," Johanna hissed as they shape-shifted back into their Seiren selves and flew into the night with their treasures clutched in their claws.

Leonard and Kathy walked quickly back toward their assigned rooms without saying a word. At that moment, Kathy would've given anything to be back home.

"Don't say anything about this to the others?" she pleaded, just outside her door. "Let's keep this our secret and get out of Orphea as fast as we can."

Leonard gave her a brief, but warm hug. She wanted to kiss him goodnight, but thought she'd better not. Instead, she turned, entered her room and locked the door, checking it twice.

Chapter Ten

While the Messengers of Music were sleeping in their beds, the proud Seirens flew across the skies of Orphea into the darkness of Dis toward the fortress to deliver their prizes to their Master. The clouds settling around the fortress towers turned from white to gray to black, soaking up the darkness from within the grim castle, then curled around the buttresses and slithered along the bottom ledges of the stone windows

The black-caped Jedermann, Master of the Seirens, stood on his outer balcony, caressing the slim relic of relics, the scepter of harmony, the Gold Baton. In his hands it had long since lost its golden shine. He tucked it away in the folds of his cape. In his youth, he had himself been good-looking and known for talent and charm. Now furrows of rage and hatred lined his drawn though still handsome face.

He scanned the sky. His winged slaves should have returned by now. His very gaze caused the lightening to crack, the thunder to roar, the Gold Baton to turn even blacker. The flashes of light revealed cat-like winged creatures blackening the sky, flying in V-formation toward the castle. Soon it would be time to begin building the stack of wood.

He walked in long strides to his inner balcony overlooking

the courtyard below. The sight filled him with satisfaction. The courtyard was filled with the lost children of Orphea, most of them running wild. Several clutched instruments in their hands, using them as make-shift weapons.

Jedermann spread his massive bat-like wings and swooped down into the courtyard. All the children and Seirens stopped what they were doing and bowed to him.

Jedermann left them to their chaos and flew to the site for the bonfire. "Build it high, my soldiers" he commanded, "for when we burn all four of their 'sacred' instruments, Orphea will be ours." The Seirens piled logs and sticks of wood into a large pile. They were all catlike creatures with extra long fangs and claws—many of them were as large as horses.

His top two Seiren commanders flew down and landed in front of their Master. They bowed on one knee before him, then stood up. They were sleek creatures with the bodies and feet of humans and the heads and front paws of cats. Amathes, the male, had the powerful head and shoulders of a striped Bengal tiger. He laid Leonard's cello at Jedermann's feet. Aplestos, the female, was slimmer, slinkier and black, with a leopard-shaped head, the size of a human's. She laid Kathy's viola next to the cello. "Two down and two to go," she said, her eyes glistening. Her long, slender cat-like body trembled as her master touched her shoulders with approval.

"Nice work, my dark ones," hissed Jedermann. "Muddled Fuddle thought his warning would be enough to prevent losing half the sacred instruments? Fool!"

He motioned for them to put the instruments on the wood pile, then Jedermann rubbed his bony hands together. "We shall have a grand burning ceremony once we have all four of the instruments. That day will signal the ultimate doom of Orphea." His Seirens cheered.

"Come with me to my music box, my commanders. We

must plan carefully." Up they flew to his tower chamber.

"Oh, Master," Aplestos said. Her deep-set black eyes shimmered, her wings quivered with excitement. "It was so easy! You should've seen the girl's eyes light up when the jewels touched her hand."

Amathes said, "That boy wasn't even close to believing in the Prophecy."

Jedermann's pride for his top Seirens grew with each passing second. He paced the polished floors of his chambers. "Oh, I can promise you that getting the other two instruments will be just as easy."

He strolled across the room and lifted the lid of his music box. As the eerie tune filled the chamber, he thoughtfully studied the images in the sound bubbles of the sleeping children and planned his next scheme.

Amathes and Aplestos sidled across the room over to the fire and stretched out on the black bear skin. "Do you remember when the Master first held the magic baton in his hands?" Aplestos whispered.

"How could any of us ever forget? The most wicked thing I've ever seen!" Amathes whispered back. "He couldn't get the hang of it. The baton was used only to bring beauty and music to life..."

"...and he wielded it to destroy!"

"He pointed the baton at the ginkgo tree and said 'DIE!'"

"Yes, I remember it well," Aplestos recalled. "But the tree instead turned into the most beautiful living thing ever seen."

They rolled around on the rug, barely able to contain their laughter. When Jedermann glanced up from his thoughts, they quickly stilled themselves.

"You find something funny, do you?" Jedermann roared. With angry fire radiating from his eyes he raised the blackened baton and blew them across the room.

Aplestos shook herself back into shape and flew to his side. "No, master, please, forgive us," she purred, rubbing her cat-like back against him, trying to appease his anger.

"Put your talents to better use than laughing at your lord and master's expense. How fortunate for all of us when I learned how to reverse the baton's powers to perform backwards, to force my will through it to kill, to destroy and deceive. Lucky for you, my power has given you all you could ask for."

Amathes and Aplestos didn't dare breathe a word.

Jedermann pointed to the images in the sound bubbles arising from the music box. "Just look at them. They think they are fulfilling their destiny. They think they're in for the time of their lives, do they?"

"More likely the *end* of their lives!" Aplestos said. "And we'll have control of everything."

Jedermann raised his eyebrows.

She added hastily, "Of course I mean you, honored one— YOU will have control of everything."

He grabbed her roughly by the chin and sneered, "Are you sure of that, my beauty?"

Amathes had to restrain himself from jumping to her rescue.

"Quite sure, my lord," she said, lowering her eyes, and rubbing her furry back against his leg.

"Good."

"Master," Amathes added. "We will have the time of our lives tempting each of those children to come to our side, and better yet," he added with a growl, "if we can't make them see things our way, the fun will really begin." His deep-throated purr revealed his excitement.

"Ah, yes, such charming thoughts, my second in command," Jedermann said and released Aplestos, who rubbed her chin and her neck, and licked her master's hand with her rough cat-tongue.

"Oh, how pleasing it will be to add them to our collection of mindless slaves out there," Aplestos said as she gazed down at the mob of children dancing wildly in the courtyard to the savage beating of a drum.

Jedermann stared deeply into one of the images from his music box. "What do you make of this one?" he asked, pointing toward Christina. She was sound asleep in the softly cushioned bed.

Jedermann

"The one who hasn't spoken?" Amathes said.

"Yes. I'm afraid she may have special telepathic powers," Jedermann admitted. "She may well be the hardest to stop, especially with her brother guarding her every move."

"You're right, Master. We can't take her too lightly," Aplestos cautioned. "She most certainly sees and hears things the others don't."

"Right you are, my dear." Jedermann's glance caused the fur to rise on the back of Amathes' neck.

"But now that we've tricked the two oldest ones out of their weapons," Aplestos said, "how will we trick the one with the spiked hair who is so sure of himself?"

"Oh, he'll not be a problem," Jedermann said. "I know his type. Impressive on the outside, but *nothing* on the inside. Easily influenced. He'll be getting into mischief with the others here soon enough—and enjoying every moment of it."

"And what about the leader, the serious one?" Amathes asked.

"Haven't you been watching him?" Jedermann responded. "Haven't you seen the fear in his eyes? You'll see what I've got in mind for him 'down the road' shall we say?"

Aplestos and Amathes licked their lips.

"I can't wait, though, until we do in Dr. Fuddle," Amathes said.

"NO!" Jedermann grabbed the Seiren by the neck and lifted him high in the air. "I, and I alone will deal with Fuddle. He's MINE." Jedermann dropped Amathes onto the floor.

"Understood, Master." Amathes landed lightly on his feet and brushed himself off. "He's all yours. But how are we going to stop those puffed up composers from protecting all of them?"

"Leave that to me," Jedermann said.

Jedermann stared at Tyler, then the others in the magic

music box's sound images. "Soon all the young people here will help us without realizing what they're doing." He reached into the deep front pocket of his cloak and produced the long, black baton.

"I possess this now and forever," he boasted with a laugh. He raised the legendary scepter of harmony high into the air. "Fuddle may have beaten me once when we were young, but he'll never have this baton again. Whoever holds the baton, holds the power. And it is mine!"

Jedermann stepped out onto the balcony and signaled to his army of Seirens to follow him. He spread his black wings and took off, his feline army following, shaping into a black cloud formation that cast a shadow over the forests and meadows and rivers on their way toward the first village.

Where the people were.

Where the children were.

Where beauty and harmony used to exist—before the darkness from the now Black Baton cut its path of destruction and decay across all of Orphea.

Chapter Eleven

As soon as Tyler opened his eyes the next morning, he sensed something was wrong. He looked around the room and saw Antonio still asleep, his drum tucked neatly next to his bedside. But Leonard was already awake, nervously looking out the window with his cello case tossed in the corner.

"Wake up, Antonio," Tyler said, "something bad happened last night. Don't you feel it, too, Leonard?"

"Uh, everything pretty much seems the same to me," Leonard mumbled. Tyler thought that Leonard's response was strange—not the usual overconfident comeback he expected.

Tyler, Antonio, and Leonard dressed and met with Christina and Kathy in the hallway. All the Messengers were holding their instruments. One of the Countess' special helpers led them to Dr. Fuddle and the Countess in a formal breakfast room.

"Good morning to all of you," Countess Thun said.

"Yes, good morning." Dr Fuddle's glance in their direction confirmed that he, too, felt something was very wrong. Even a tasty breakfast of Penderecki Pancakes topped with Berg

Blueberries and Stravinsky Syrup couldn't stop the rising tide of anxiety in the room.

Suddenly the doors burst open. Into the room ran a young man, panic-stricken and panting, "Dr. Fuddle! Dr. Fuddle!"

An elderly butler hurried after the intruder and wheezed, "My apologies, Countess Thun, but I couldn't stop him."

"It's all right, Manfred," Countess Thun said and looked at Dr. Fuddle with fear in her eyes.

"Catch your breath, sir," Dr. Fuddle said. "Here, my good man, drink some water, then tell us what has happened."

"Our worst fears have been confirmed, Dr. Fuddle. The leader of the enemy himself has made an appearance with his army in my village of Adagio on the other side of the hill. He has grown bolder and even more dangerous!"

Everyone gasped.

Kathy and Leonard exchanged uneasy glances, knowing how hard it would be for them now to try to break away from the others to leave Orphea.

The man continued. "Right in plain daylight in the town square, he cast some sort of spell upon our children who followed him out of town as if they were in a trance—as if he were the Pied Piper. My own son..." he broke down, head in hands, shoulders shaking in grief. "When we tried to stop them, we couldn't move; they put a spell on us too. We were like statues."

"Who, man, who is this leader?" Dr. Fuddle urged him, lifting him up.

"I don't know. I don't know. Long black cape..."

Dr. Fuddle frowned. "I'll be back directly." He left the room and returned with a painting that he showed to the father. It was a portrait of two young men, dressed in fine clothes standing beside a grand piano. The gold plaque beneath read *The Grande Piano Competition.*

The father pointed to the man on the left. "Yes, that's the one, the leader of our enemies, only he's much older and looks more frightening now."

"It is as I feared—Jedermann." Dr. Fuddle slammed his fist into the palm of his hand, and stomped to the other end of the room.

"Wow, we've never seen him angry before," Antonio whispered.

"It's his old rival," Countess Thun said.

"There's something else," the young father hesitated.

Dr. Fuddle collected himself and walked back toward them.

"He's got...they've all got wings. Terrible huge black wings! They fly!"

"That means Jedermann's powers in black magic have indeed grown much stronger."

"Oh, dear Dr. Fuddle, whatever shall we do?" Countess Thun cried.

"We must leave immediately." Dr. Fuddle looked distressed and motioned to the elderly butler, "the coach, please."

"Thank you, dear Countess, for your gracious hospitality." He embraced her warmly. "Come, Messengers of Music, we haven't a moment to lose."

"Stay close to Dr. Fuddle, my young friends," called the Countess as they climbed into the coach. "And don't let anything distract you."

Dr. Fuddle waved to the Countess. He glanced up to the driver of the coach and said, "To the Albrechtsberger Conservatory of Music."

Kathy pulled on Leonard's sleeve, frowning at him. He knew she wanted him to ask Dr. Fuddle to turn back, to return them to the safety of the Golden Doors because it would be their last chance. He shook his head no. All the others, except Antonio, sensed the risk that lay ahead of them.

Antonio, unaware of the damages they were in, said, "I still don't see exactly how our instruments can protect us and defeat the bad guys. What could I do with this drum? Bang them over the head with it? Poke their eyes out with the drumsticks?" Everyone was glad to have an excuse to laugh.

"Remember how those cursed kids ran when they heard the music? The music has some sort of power over them," Tyler said.

"That's right, Tyler. And you'll see just how much power it has soon," Dr. Fuddle replied.

As the stagecoach moved along the path, the morning sun shone brightly. But dark clouds hovered in the distance over the mountains. The Messengers noticed the path began to climb into the mountains. The view was amazing, but Kathy and Leonard's wrecked nerves cast an awkward tension inside the coach. They'd barely slept the night before and keeping their secret from their friends was feeling like a task too big for either of them.

Leonard remained quiet but Kathy was anxious, jumping out of her skin with every little noise. She clung tightly to her purse, as if the bracelet would fly out to expose her horrible deed. At one point, she became excessively chatty, commenting on every little thing they passed and pointing it out to Christina.

"Now that Jedermann has gained such great power, I fear that many of our prized pupils may have defected and joined his forces," Dr. Fuddle said. "It is a blessing we have our Messengers of Music on our side," he smiled at Kathy and Leonard, who squirmed and said nothing.

Soon the stagecoach came to a stop in front of a massive stone gate, which read:

THE ALBRECHTSBERGER CONSERVATORY

A scholarly man with tiny spectacles greeted them at the front doors. "A good day to you," he said.

"Professor Czerny, please meet our Messengers of Music," Dr. Fuddle said. He turned to the Messengers, "This is Professor Carl Czerny, one of our most famous teachers. As a former student of Beethoven, he in turn taught the great Franz Liszt, whom you will meet later." Dr. Fuddle introduced everyone.

"The pleasure is mine," Professor Czerny smiled. "Please come in." He turned his attention to Dr. Fuddle. "Our security forces have captured more of the Seirens, but their powers are stronger. They're being held in the secret chambers underground."

"You mean you've really got some of those monsters here?" Antonio asked.

"Some of them," replied the professor. "Soon you'll see them for yourself."

Antonio seemed to be the only one excited at the prospect of the captured Seirens.

Dr. Fuddle led them deep inside the Conservatory. "Come, my friends. There's much for you to learn and we have little time to prepare."

Christina was staring at Kathy's purse. She thought she sensed movement as she followed Dr. Fuddle, Professor Czerny, and the others into a spacious entry hall.

Professor Czerny led the Messengers into a winding series of hallways, with large rehearsal halls beyond each door. Tyler spotted a group of youngsters in a brass ensemble playing music fit for a queen. Across the hallway, Kathy saw an ensemble of young women singing music *a cappella*—with no musical accompaniment, as if they were preparing for a royal wedding.

The sounds of music brought a smile to Dr. Fuddle's face, but he kept a close eye on Kathy and Leonard. He knew something had happened, that they were hiding something.

"And here is the practice wing," Dr. Fuddle said. Beautiful exciting music sounded from all directions. Hundreds of small rooms contained students practicing on every kind of instrument. Tyler, Christina and Antonio ran from room to room, peering through the windows. Tyler looked around in amazement. "This is exciting! It's like hearing every instrument in the world at the same time."

"Wow, look at her," Antonio said. A girl who looked about Kathy's age sat at a piano, drilling a thunderous cascade of octaves over and over. "That sounds fierce."

"Our students work non-stop," Professor Czerny stated. "And those remaining are motivated to work harder than ever, preparing to face what is ahead."

"How many are still here?" Tyler asked.

"About half," Czerny replied. "The others have already been lured over to the dark side."

"That's terrible," Christina wrote. Tyler shuddered.

"That's why our task is so urgent," Dr. Fuddle said. "Come."

Soon the sounds of drums and other instruments reverberated outside a large-windowed door where dozens of percussionists and keyboard players practiced inside a massive room. A sign above the door read: "The Cage Concert Center for Modern Music."

"Wow!" Antonio said. "I didn't know there'd be so many drummers in a place like this!"

"Of course, Antonio," said Dr. Fuddle. "We embrace all forms of music. Our only requirements are quality, discipline and a commitment to excellence."

"And nothing short of excellence is what we must have— especially now," Professor Czerny added.

Kathy and Leonard stood back from the others. Dr. Fuddle

noticed the jarring impact the musical sounds had on them compared to Tyler, Antonio and Christina.

"We have one more stop," Dr. Fuddle said, looking directly to Leonard who felt singled out. Kathy noticed and moved a few paces away from him.

Dr. Fuddle and Professor Czerny led them out of the practice wing and down another hall to an open door with a sign reading:

INSTRUMENTS OF ANTIQUITY

"Everyone, observe," Dr. Fuddle said. "The music of this unusual instrument is known to prompt all sorts of extreme reactions."

Antonio elbowed Tyler. "Look, there she is again," he pointed to Mozart's sister Nannerl, who sat at a very strange looking musical device. Students were seated in front of her holding an assortment of instruments.

"She's about to perform on a glass harmonica," Dr. Fuddle said. He motioned for Kathy and Leonard to stand closer to the demonstration.

The instrument looked unlike any harmonica any of the friends had ever seen. It stood on a shiny, mahogany frame with a small bench in front of it, much like a piano seat. The instrument itself consisted of thirty-seven glass bowls varying in size from small to large, stacked on their sides around a central metal rotating rod.

"The glass harmonica was invented by Benjamin Franklin," Professor Czerny added. "Legend has it, that the sounds of the glass harmonica can have many effects on a person and in rare cases, it can even invoke insanity with its overwhelming beauty. Watch and listen to see what kind of effect it has on you."

Dr. Fuddled gazed at Leonard, hoping the music might prompt a verbal clue for his and Kathy's odd behavior.

Nannerl arranged the students to perform the unusual

opening, then she began to play the curious instrument. Her wet fingers appeared propelled by invisible wings, fluttering wildly on the strange contraption and causing her voluminous wig to bounce in unison with her movements. Her focus never left the music while she continually dipped her pearly hands into a water-filled bowl, moving them rapidly back onto the grooves of the revolving, multi-colored glass bowls, faster than seemed humanly possible.

The odd sounds bore into Leonard's mind like a drill. He felt as if he were *really* about to go insane. Kathy fidgeted nervously. She felt as if she wanted to confess what she and Leonard had done the night before. Something about the musical sounds moved her emotionally like no music had ever moved her before. The sweetness made her feel an unbearable guilt about wanting to leave Orphea and their mission there.

Awestruck, Christina witnessed the creation of these unearthly, pristine sounds and for an instant felt like she was reliving the wonderful episode in Dr. Fuddle's plant-filled conservatory. And then, as magically as the music had begun, it ended.

She suddenly stared at Kathy's purse again and thought to herself: *something bad is in there!* She nudged Tyler to point it out, but just then Dr. Fuddle and Professor Czerny urged them forward.

"Quite astonishing, wouldn't you say?" Dr. Fuddle said. "Music has power to affect us on such a profound level." He waited to see if Kathy or Leonard would comment, but they stood silent, relieved that the music had stopped.

"I've never heard *anything* like that," Antonio said.

"Me either," Tyler added.

Dr. Fuddle and Professor Czerny led them down another long hallway, passing many doors bearing the names of famous composers. When they reached another set of double doors, Professor Czerny opened them and said, "I'm off to teach my students. Study the music you'll hear. It possesses a power even brighter than the light of the sun—a power that can penetrate the deepest darkness, a power that no force in the universe can destroy. Mark my words, and commit yourselves to greatness." He smiled, turned, and walked back down the long hallway.

Dr. Fuddle led his new pupils into what looked like a university classroom and arranged them on a large stage. "What you learn here will be your weapon against the enemy. Listen as if your life depends upon it—because it does."

Tyler Harrington

Chapter Twelve

Tyler could feel everything he was seeing and hearing at the Albrechtsberger Conservatory becoming a part of him, just as Dr. Fuddle had predicted. But he felt nervous at the same time that he would be forced to try to make music happen. He couldn't bear the possibility of failure.

"Now, take your instruments out of their cases," Dr. Fuddle instructed.

Kathy felt paranoid and uncomfortable opening her viola case and kept looking down at her purse. Twice she thought of opening it to see if the bracelet was still there, but she couldn't bring herself to look.

Doors opened in the back and in filed Johann Sebastian Bach, his wife and all their children with instruments in hand. Leonard glanced at Kathy as soon as he saw Johann Christoph and Johanna.

"There they are," Kathy whispered.

The Bach family walked right by them, smiling, and took their places in a chamber orchestra arrangement surrounding a harpsichord.

"They look different than they did in that room last night," Kathy said.

"They sure do," Leonard said in a hushed tone. "More like they did when we first met them in the banquet hall."

Johanna looked directly at Kathy with a friendly smile, without the slightest sign of that frightening spark in her eyes that Kathy had seen the night before. Anna Magdalena positioned herself at the harpsichord. Johann Christoph smiled brightly, assisting his younger sister with her music stand.

Kathy suddenly felt disoriented. She could have sworn she felt a twitch at her side. Christina noticed Kathy's discomfort. Tyler sensed something very odd, as if the energy of the room had shifted. He'd felt things like that his whole life, always knowing they meant something.

"Tyler, please come center stage," Dr. Fuddle said.

Tyler stood and came forward with his French horn. His insides churned at this moment of truth. He fought the fear welling up inside of him—the fear that he might not measure up, reliving his reasons for never wanting to study piano with his mother.

"Now begins the work, young warrior," Dr. Fuddle declared. Tyler breathed through his nose deeply, resisting the urge to count. "Begin by removing the mouthpiece and blow through it like this, concentrating on a single note." Dr. Fuddle demonstrated on his own mouthpiece. "Now sit up straight and support the air stream from your diaphragm." Dr. Fuddle glowed with enthusiasm, relishing his teaching despite such dire circumstances.

Tyler sat up and lowered his jaw as Dr. Fuddle had done, took a very deep breath and attempted to duplicate Dr. Fuddle's demonstration. The first attempt sounded feeble and off key.

Leonard shot Kathy a quick look as if to say, *I told you the instruments aren't special*. But Kathy was watching Tyler and didn't notice Leonard.

"Not bad for a first try," Dr. Fuddle cheered. "Now try again, keeping your feet flat on the floor and match my pitch."

I can do this. I can do this, Tyler thought. After several attempts he produced a remarkably clear tone. He was shocked and pleased and only wished his mother could've witnessed his first attempt to make music, something she had always hoped for him.

"Now put the mouthpiece back on the horn and I'll teach you three notes," Dr. Fuddle said, before demonstrating. Tyler repeated the tones precisely. "Now you must drill and practice making the 'f' 'g' and 'a' notes hundreds of times each."

One of Bach's children assisted him to a practice chair at the far end of the stage. Christina had never felt prouder for her brother.

"Next, Antonio come forward with your drum," Dr. Fuddle said, motioning him to where Tyler had been seated. "I'm sure you will learn this in short order."

Antonio, seeing that Tyler had learned quickly, eagerly took his position. Dr. Fuddle showed him exactly how to sit, how to hold the drum sticks and wrote out very simple rhythms for him to practice.

"All right!" Antonio shouted, successful on the first try.

Before long Antonio had progressed to an amazing degree of skill. "Just wait 'til the guys back home see me," he boasted and followed Johanna to Tyler's area for further drilling and instruction.

"Now Kathy and Leonard, it is your turn to come forward," Dr. Fuddle instructed, pulling two chairs to the left center. "We will do this slightly differently for you. Herr Bach will conduct a movement of a concerto with two of his children. You Leonard must study carefully every movement of the cellist and Kathy, you the violist. After which time I'll teach you a precise set of drills until you master a simple scale."

Tyler and Antonio were so impressed by their own two-man band they paid little attention to Bach's demonstration. Christina watched Leonard and Kathy nervously, feeling something wasn't right.

Then Bach raised his arms to conduct. "Now, let's begin the performance. One and two and three and four…"

Kathy tensely watched the young violist fearing that somehow her secret would cause something to go wrong. By the time Bach finished conducting, she felt completely unnerved. She kept glancing at Leonard in panic throughout the movement, wondering how they could explain being able to play their instruments so well without any instruction. And when it was time for her to play her viola, her nightmare really began. Dr. Fuddle showed her carefully how to hold the instrument and use the bow. But her hands shook violently with every note she attempted to play.

At first, Dr. Fuddle tried to ignore what was happening, but as Kathy's panic mounted, and she kept trying to play without any results of any kind, it grew impossible.

Leonard now felt panicked, too. He'd seen Kathy play the instrument perfectly the night before. When it was his turn, he fumbled his bow over the strings of his cello, creating nothing but nerve-wracking screeches.

Bach brought the music lesson to an abrupt halt. Suddenly all eyes were focused on Kathy and Leonard. Even Tyler and Antonio stopped their playing and came forward to see what was happening.

"I…I…I…don't know what's wrong," she mumbled, mortified. "I just can't seem to play a single note."

Bach shot a glance toward Dr. Fuddle. He knew they both suspected Kathy's instrument was a counterfeit, although it appeared exactly like the sacred viola. He asked her to try again.

"Leonard," she insisted, "try yours again first. Maybe our strings have stretched or something."

Leonard tried to play but stopped after a few shrill sounds.

"Evidently something is making our instruments stop working," he said. "Or maybe teaching us how to play is much harder than anyone thought."

At that moment, Christina looked at Kathy's purse. This time she knew she saw something moving inside of it.

"Yes, that must be what's happened," Kathy said. "What should we do?"

Dr. Fuddle's troubled expression triggered a painful stab of guilt in both Kathy and Leonard.

Somehow he knows what's happened, Leonard thought.

"Let me see that cello," Dr. Fuddle said.

Leonard handed him the cello and his uneasiness increased. His heart pounded.

Bach took a hard look at the cello and shook his head.

After several moments Dr. Fuddle placed it onto the floor. He motioned for Kathy's viola for closer inspection.

"These are not the instruments we gave you," Dr. Fuddle said, finally placing the viola on the floor next to the cello.

"But how?" Anna asked. "They've been in safe hands all along."

Kathy and Leonard both felt a powerful pang of guilt as Dr. Fuddle, Bach and Anna conferred. And just as Leonard opened his mouth to confess what had really happened, he saw Kathy's desperate glance. The pleading in her eyes kept him from speaking.

"We *will* get to the bottom of this," Dr. Fuddle announced. "These instruments are counterfeit."

Kathy brushed her shoulder, thinking it was her nerves twitching, but then felt the movement inside her purse become stronger. She looked down in horror. The leather bag trembled, the straps wiggling. She threw it off her shoulder and dropped it. It landed with a loud thud on the floor.

Everyone was startled by the sound. Their eyes were drawn to the strange sight on the stage floor. The purse writhed, pulsating from side to side until it began to thrash violently. Then suddenly it stopped. No one moved. Slowly a hideous green head worked its way from the opening of the purse. The girls screamed as a snake, in the exact rainbow colors as the bracelet, slithered its way out of the bag, arched its back, and headed toward Kathy.

"GREED!" it hissed wickedly into her face, "GRRREEEEEDD!" The serpent quickly streaked across the floor, off the stage, and disappeared through the wall at the opposite side of the room.

The girls screaming and the brisk departure of the snake caused chaos to overtake the scene until Dr. Fuddle's tapping of his pointed baton managed to bring everything under control.

Leonard grabbed the purse off the floor and threw it as far as he could away from the stage.

"I never want to see that thing again!" Kathy screamed with tears streaming down her face. "I'm so sorry for what I've done."

Leonard leaped up, pointing to Johann Christoph and Johanna and exclaimed, "They forced us to trade instruments with them last night!" He then went on to explain how the trade took place, leaving out a few details.

Johann stood to his feet. "What are you talking about?"

"Don't try to deny it!" Kathy yelled.

"We would never do such a thing," Johanna said. "Father never made such promises to us."

Everyone spoke at once until Dr. Fuddle brought the commotion to a halt. "There is a very obvious explanation for this," he said, disappointment streaming from his eyes.

"This is clearly the work of Jedermann and his Seirens. You

were deceived," Bach explained to Leonard and Kathy.

"Because you did not believe, we've lost half our arsenal," Johann shouted.

"I'm so sorry, Dr. Fuddle. I don't know what more I can say," Kathy sobbed, falling into Leonard's embrace.

"And I'm sorry, too," Leonard said. "I was a fool to go against my instincts." He hung his head in shame.

Tyler stepped forward. "What good are your apologies now? You know if one of us fails, the mission fails."

Tyler started to say more, but Dr. Fuddle stopped him.

"Please," Anna said. "I beg all of you to be on guard at all times. You must do exactly as you're told."

"Tell us immediately if you suspect something is wrong," Bach warned.

"Unfortunately," Dr. Fuddle said gravely, "this is only the beginning of the deceptive, manipulative tricks that will be raised against us. But we *will* get your instruments back. We must."

Kathy broke from Leonard, wiping the tears from her face. "I have to make up for what I've done."

Dr. Fuddle paused. "Let this be a lesson of the dangers to come."

Chapter Thirteen

Their guilt drove all thoughts of abandoning Orphea and the mission from Kathy and Leonard's minds. They opened their hearts to Dr. Fuddle and the music, hoping to recapture his trust and their friends' respect. After much practice, they had mastered the basic movements on the substitute viola and cello Bach had provided for them.

"With even more hard work, you'll be able to play all sorts of music at least adequately," Dr. Fuddle told them.

Bach circled around them, instructing the Messengers on their drills over and over. "Number Twelve. Exercise number twelve fifty times. Kathy, please relax your shoulder and arms. Let the bow glide with ease."

Dr. Fuddle studied the new music pupils. He knew the dangers they faced now loomed larger than ever in all their minds, even in his own mind. He watched Tyler the closest of all, and saw what increased his young student's fears—namely his fear that he had nothing close to the courage needed to fulfill his destined mission.

For what seemed like weeks, as darkness and destruction continued to encroach across the land of Orphea, the

Messengers of Music followed the precise instructions of Dr. Fuddle and Bach, until they'd mastered reading musical notation, acquired amazing levels of technique, and accomplished what would have taken many years of disciplined work otherwise. Tyler and his friends remembered that Dr. Fuddle had told them that this "shortcut" to excellence could only happen in Orphea under the dreadful circumstances they faced.

"Now we must proceed to the Lowlands," Dr. Fuddle said mysteriously. Following a temporary farewell to Bach and his musical family, he led them out of the Conservatory, into the carriage and back onto the path.

Kathy recalled what Countess Thun said about the Lowlands earlier and her mind filled with anxiety. *I hope we never see any more of those flying Seiren creatures, she thought.*

"What *are* the Lowlands?" Tyler asked.

"An area of Orphea that has been completely destroyed," Dr. Fuddle answered, "an area of our enemy's harshest victories. Only there you'll acquire the final musical skills necessary to protect yourself against the Seirens."

Soon the horses slowed as the path descended steeply. Once they reached the lowest stretch, the forest became uncomfortably dense. To Tyler the darkness felt like giant arms reaching out to grab them. Seeing more than a few yards ahead became impossible. The dark green branches dimmed the comforting sunlight and before long, the foliage turned into strange, grotesque formations, blocking the sun out almost completely. They were surrounded by an eerie semi-darkness.

Dr. Fuddle stopped and turned around to warn them, "As we enter the Lowlands, I insist you stay near each other and hold tightly to the instruments. It's far worse here than anything you've seen till now."

The magic of Orphea faded more and more depressingly

around each bend. Even the bird calls they'd heard all along had ceased. Never once, in all his life, had Tyler seen such a look of alarm in his sister's eyes.

"We must proceed on foot from here." Dr. Fuddle's face radiated inspiration in spite of the surroundings.

Tyler put his arm around Christina.

As they approached the Lowlands, an opening appeared among the dense trees. The remains of a once park-like village bore testimony to the power of Jedermann's invasion. Crumbled fountains now contained putrid water.

Christina pointed at a wilted water lily. "Don't touch that water!" Dr. Fuddle intervened before her hand could reach for the flower. "It may contain disease," he explained. "That stench is the smell of decay. If we fail to act quickly, soon all of Orphea will look like this."

"Is it safe for anyone to even enter here?" Tyler asked.

He and the others looked around and saw that every living thing had been killed—even the trees had been stripped of all their leaves.

"Yes, it's safe for now. Our guards have scoured the area and are convinced the Seirens are finished here. There's nothing more for them to destroy." Dr. Fuddle's expression grew darker with his next words. "It happened very gradually. No one noticed at first, but once they did, it was too late for this village. Subtle progress is what makes Jedermann and his fiends so dangerous in the first place. He's cunning and clever. He works unceasingly while people are off guard and unaware. I'm sure if you think about your home on the earthly realm, you've seen similar examples of destruction."

Leonard recalled seeing his father shaking his head observing events throughout the world—terrorists, revolutions, wars. Kathy thought of the destruction of the rain forests and Tyler thought of the violence that occurred even in their own town.

He thought of the bullying and vandalism in his neighborhood, much like the destructive behavior of the boys in that first cursed village they had seen. The disharmony that threatened Orphea was affecting earth as well. He worried about Antonio's other friends, hoping Antonio wouldn't give in to their peer pressure.

Dr. Fuddle's face showed even more concern. "We've studied their tactics continuously. Jedermann and his Seirens must be confronted on all levels." Dr. Fuddle had never looked more serious. "If we fail, all will be lost."

We will not fail, Tyler thought, feeling a surge of internal strength. *To succeed is our destiny.* He looked at Christina's pure innocence and never felt more determined in his life.

Dr. Fuddle steered them toward an imposing building and frowned to see its ancient doors ripped from their hinges, lying broken in the street. Makeshift wooden doors had been pounded up hastily. He looked at Christina, glad to see that she'd regained her calm expression. "Come with me inside," he said, leading them into the structure. Several guards in green uniforms stood at attention against the inside walls. "Greetings, does everything remain under control here?" Dr. Fuddle questioned the guards.

"Yes," the tallest guard said. "He's making continuous breakthroughs."

"Who's 'he'?" Leonard asked.

"A top scientist has been recruited to head our research team." Dr. Fuddle looked directly at Leonard.

Passing the guards they walked past damaged paintings of great composers. A spray-painted moustache disfigured one stately gentleman's face. Another had its eyes gouged out.

"The Seirens did this?" Tyler asked.

"No," Dr. Fuddle answered. "This crime was committed by the young people of Orphea, incited by the Seirens. They were hypnotized by promises." He looked at Kathy and Leonard. "But don't become disheartened. It may be too late here, but there's much goodness left in Orphea."

Enough goodness to beat this? Tyler wondered.

Dr. Fuddle led the way down a lengthy corridor, passing more guards, before reaching an enormous vault with three numbered dials on its door. He turned the dial in the middle clockwise.

"Sixteen-eighty-five" he said quietly to himself. Then he turned a second dial counterclockwise: "1732." And then the third clockwise: "1756, 1770." Everyone watched closely, listening to the numbers. "1797, 1809, 1810, 1811." Cling, ring, click. "1833." And then after several additional numbers a loud ding sounded, and the door opened.

"How do you remember all those numbers?" Tyler asked.

"They are the earthly birth dates of composers," Dr. Fuddle replied. "Bach in 1685, Haydn in 1732, Mozart in 1756, Beethoven in 1770 and so on. Now, right this way."

Suddenly the air was filled with a disgusting odor that made it almost unbearable to breathe.

"Pee-euww!" Kathy complained, holding her nose. "I hope that smell doesn't get into my clothes." Leonard rolled his eyes. "They're all I have."

Dr. Fuddle led them into a square room with burnished steel walls. A small winding staircase descended from its center. "We must go below."

One by one, carefully holding their instruments, they followed him down the narrow steps. Due to the size of his cello, Leonard had the most trouble, but managed to hold it upright through the downward spiral.

"What in the world?" Tyler said when they reached a room with concrete walls, lined with concrete shelves holding huge black containers. Even the ceiling was concrete. "What's in those containers?"

106

"Come and see," Dr. Fuddle said. He opened a box stacked full with dozens of small reed instruments. "These are the easiest instruments to manufacture on short notice. Follow me and you'll understand their purpose."

He led them across the room and into a long passageway extending far into the distance. The passageway was lined with vaulted doors with thick windows. They stopped and peered through the first window. Inside, men in white laboratory coats wearing plastic gloves labored at humming machines.

"All materials are being carefully tested in these rooms before being sent to other rooms to be manufactured into instruments," Dr. Fuddle explained. "Then once the instruments are proven usable, they're placed into shipping carriers and distributed to all the citizens of Orphea." Dr. Fuddle led them past the manufacturing rooms through a set of glass doors.

At the far end of the room stood a man with bushy gray hair, facing away from them. He was busily working at a machine with wires extending in all directions connecting it to video monitors set up on a metal table. Other men studied the monitors, writing notes.

"We're here," Dr. Fuddle announced.

The man turned around. At the sight of his black moustache Leonard blinked his eyes in disbelief.

"It can't be! Einstein?" Leonard said, and immediately corrected himself. "You're Professor Einstein?!"

"That I am," Professor Einstein responded, smiling at the Messengers. "I've been looking forward to your arrival."

Dr. Fuddle winked at Kathy, seeing her reaction to meeting the famous composers. He then introduced each Messenger to the Professor.

"Are you surprised at our equipment after all you've seen in your father's lab, Leonard?" Professor Einstein said. "I'm a true admirer of your father's work. The Nobel Prize in biochemistry is an honor few have attained, my boy."

"I'm pleased to meet you," Leonard said, "But what are you doing here?"

"I was called to Orphea by Sebastian Bach," he began. "When informed of the urgency of the situation, I came immediately."

"That's right," Dr. Fuddle said. "Aside from being the father of modern physics and awarded the Nobel Prize, Professor Einstein became an accomplished violinist during his youth and remained a great fan of classical music throughout his lifetime."

"Indeed," he said. "I didn't think twice about becoming involved. My admiration for the compositions of Sebastian Bach and Amadeus Mozart is well known and I wanted to help prevent this great kingdom of music from falling to ruin."

"Please be seated," Dr. Fuddle said to the Messengers.

"I must brace you for what you are about to see," Einstein began. "I assure you we are being as humane as possible."

"Absolutely," Dr. Fuddle agreed. "Professor Einstein and our composers are dedicated to studying the Seirens, but never resorting to cruelty."

Tyler shifted in his chair.

"Don't worry, the Seirens have been safely contained. We've been able to capture six of them during the rampage of the Lowland villages," Einstein explained. "We think we have a good map of their genetics and excellent knowledge of their physical responses to musical stimuli."

Dr. Fuddle motioned for a guard to bring a specimen dish to the table with a rubber membrane stretched across its surface. Tiny flakes of gold dust were sprinkled on the membrane.

"But before you see the Seirens on the screens," Einstein said, "we're now going to demonstrate how music can affect even an inanimate object. Watch." He nodded at Dr. Fuddle.

Dr. Fuddle reached into the pocket to produce his lyre and played a short sequence of sounds. To the Messengers' astonishment, the gold dust formed beautiful geometric patterns on the rubber membrane. With each phrase of his performance, Dr. Fuddle's music moved the gold dust until he was satisfied with the perfect six-pointed star formation.

"Amazing," Tyler said.

"And now observe this," Dr. Fuddle placed a wilted rose in a glass vase and motioned for a violinist to play one long sustained tone. Before everyone's eyes the delicate petals exploded with color. The rose was reacting to the music.

By the time the violinist had finished the first musical phrase, Tyler and Christina looked at each other, knowing each was thinking the same thing—how much they were reminded of their mother's prize-winning gardens.

Dr. Fuddle knew they were ready for the next step in their education on the transformative powers of music. "Is everyone ready for the Seirens?"

Kathy's eyes grew wide.

"I'm ready!" Antonio said.

Tyler didn't answer, but reached for Christina's hand.

Chapter Fourteen

The time had come to see the Seirens at close range. The band of Messengers wasn't at all sure about this particular phase of their mission. They squirmed in their seats.

Professor Einstein switched on the monitor and pulled two microphones toward him and Dr. Fuddle.

The screen blinked, revealing a large, brightly lit room filled with musicians tuning their musical instruments.

"Can everyone hear me?" Professor Einstein asked into his microphone.

"We read you," a strong voice answered through a speaker.

"Slowly reveal the compartments," Dr. Fuddle said, instructing an unseen technician. "Each Seiren is hearing musical tones which will keep them in a neutral state."

Gradually the monitor revealed glass compartments inside enclosed cubicles, separated by concrete walls. It almost looked like an exhibit at a zoo.

"Zoom in on Seiren Number Six," Einstein instructed.

Slowly a panther-like creature appeared on the screen.

"I'm warning you," Dr. Fuddle said, "this one isn't pretty."

The moment the Seiren came into clear focus, Kathy let out a loud gasp.

Tyler wriggled in his chair. "Look at those claws!" he said.

"It's worse than the ones that took Juliet and Elizabeth!" Antonio shouted.

"It's ghastly!" Kathy agreed. "Simply ghastly!"

"I like cats, but this is the ugliest cat I've ever seen," Leonard said.

"Most of the Seirens are far from pleasing to the eyes," Professor Einstein said. "Especially the four-legged ones who have not yet evolved. Some of them become much more human and even beautiful, believe it or not—especially the Seirens that stand on two legs in nearly humanized bodies."

"Those are the smartest and most dangerous, too," Dr. Fuddle added. "We've been unable to capture any of that level. You saw two of them seize our friends in Countess Thun's garden."

Christina shuddered at the memory.

"Number Six" strapped in its giant chair, appeared to be in a trance. Wires sprang from its feline head. Even the shoulders, arm-like wings, and paws were connected to strange devices. Its eyes were gray and cloudy.

"Notice the monitors above us," Einstein said, pointing to two more screens he'd turned on with a remote control device.

"Play an A440 pitch," Dr. Fuddle instructed one of the musicians.

A man with a violin came into view and played the pitch into a microphone.

Suddenly the Seiren's wings flared under the straps.

"All right. Stop," Einstein said.

The creature relaxed and returned to its nap-like state.

"What exactly is going on in there?" Tyler asked.

"Musical pitch is a vibration," Dr. Fuddle explained. "The

pitch we just heard is what is known as the standard concert pitch. On a piano, it is the 'A' above middle 'C'."

"And pitch," Einstein said, "is the perceived frequency of a sound. The frequency of the sound is measured in what we call hertz. Four hundred forty indicates the number of vibrations per second, in this case 440 hertz. Although we certainly don't have time now to explore the complex mathematical equations regarding the vibration of sound, there are certain things you need to know in relation to these Seirens." He looked to Dr. Fuddle to continue.

"Our esteemed composers have worked closely with Professor Einstein," Dr. Fuddle said. "They've performed thousands of experiments already to understand how each Seiren reacts to sound. And I'm happy to tell you we've made rapid progress in discovering a very crucial bit of information." Dr. Fuddle smiled broadly. "Tell them the good news, Professor Einstein."

"In a nutshell, these beasts have a weakness for certain types of musical vibrations." He smiled. "Various combinations of sounds can render them anywhere from a partial state of paralysis to being repulsed and running away. Some Seirens even become calm and receptive to our music, craving states of ecstasy. We can use this for our benefit if we play the right music."

"Wow," Leonard said. "That's absolutely staggering. I had no idea music could be so powerful on a physical level."

"Boy, what a break," Tyler said.

"It's not quite so simple," Einstein said. "You see, the problem is the sheer number of Seirens that Jedermann has spawned, all varying in power. And that's not to mention their master, whose power far surpasses the strongest of them all. The number of Seirens may well be in the thousands."

"So how and when are we going to kill them off?" Antonio asked.

"Our goal may well be *not* to kill any of them," Dr. Fuddle explained, "but to transform them into gentle, peaceful creatures through musical sounds."

Leonard looked stunned. "But what are they biologically?"

"We're not exactly sure," Einstein admitted. "From what we can tell by studying their features, they are similar to ancient saber-toothed tigers. Much is not understood about these beasts, but let's proceed to our most important discoveries. One of our first musical experiments involved seeing how these creatures responded to various arrangements of notes in a scale-based melody."

"Play a chromatic scale," Einstein said to a violinist. He turned to the Messengers to remind them that a chromatic scale has twelve notes, each a half step apart.

The Seiren's wings moved violently upon hearing the scale.

"Now, watch this," Dr. Fuddle said. He spoke into the microphone. "Play a major scale, stopping on the seventh."

"You mean the tonic sol-fa scale we learned: do, re, mi, fa, so, la, ti, but stopping before the next 'do'?" Tyler asked.

"Exactly," Dr. Fuddle looked pleased that Tyler had learned so well.

Seven notes of the scale sounded over the speakers. The Seiren's eyes bulged. It began to salivate.

"Now resolve onto the tonic."

"If I remember, that means to play the next 'do' so the scale feels complete and sounds good to the ear," Antonio announced.

Dr. Fuddle smiled broadly at his bright young student, "That's right."

When eight notes of the scale were played, the creature's eyes relaxed. Its wings settled to its sides.

"If the sequence of notes is unresolved, that is, not all eight notes are played, the creature turns violent," continued Dr.

Fuddle. "But once the sound resolves, it becomes very still, as you could see. This isn't too surprising, considering how certain types of music can produce uncontrollable behavior in humans."

"We've carefully documented the reaction of all six creatures to the standard twelve notes in the common system of tuning—known as the tempered scale, played by twelve different musicians on a total of twenty four instruments," Einstein said.

"What we've concluded, however, is that the creatures respond positively to consonance and negatively to dissonance," Dr. Fuddle said. "Consonant intervals are what sound good to our ears and dissonant intervals are what sound bad."

"Now watch how the creature responds to the consonant and dissonant intervals. Bring in the second violinist," Einstein said.

The Seiren, in its trancelike state, remained still while the two violinists performed consonant intervals, combinations pleasing to the ears. But they thrashed aggressively upon hearing the clashing tones of dissonant intervals.

"Now watch this," Dr. Fuddle said. "Perform the tritone."

When the violinists played an eerie, highly suspenseful discordant interval the Seiren collapsed limply onto its chair.

Dr. Fuddle and Einstein stood. "Now the other variable is the human variable," Einstein went on. "When considering these creatures' reactions to musical sounds, we must take into consideration not only the sounds themselves, but the harmonic energy of the person performing on the instrument, the vibrational energy of the person who built the instrument—*and* to make it even more complicated, the vibrational energy of the composer of the music."

Tyler digested the information, while the others looked confused.

"We know this is extremely complex and hard to under-stand," Dr Fuddle said, "but we can simplify our observations in a single sentence: music has power over living and nonliving matter."

"I have no doubt that is proven," Einstein said.

Tyler looked at Christina. She nodded her head in full agreement.

"Now," Einstein said, leading to the door beyond the monitors, "we must show you what all of this has to do with your purpose. Come with us into the chambers containing the creatures."

Terror swept across Kathy's face. "What exactly did you mean by 'into the chambers?' Surely we're not going near them?"

"We're very near them, Kathy," Dr. Fuddle said. "They're just beyond this door."

"They are?" Tyler asked. "Let's see them." He stood with his French horn, ready for action.

The sight and smell of the captive Seirens unnerved the Messengers. Most of them resembled some form of cat, but with their teeth and claws protruding so threateningly, they appeared far from the household variety. Musical guards armed with cellos surrounded the room. The friends moved to the far wall, to be as far away as possible from the creatures. Only one of the Seirens was strapped to a chair, the one that appeared the most vicious. The first two appeared to be passed out on the floor of their compartment; others stood with their scowling faces pressed against the glass windows.

"Can they talk?" Tyler asked.

"Possibly," Dr. Fuddle said. "But none of these have done so yet."

"Now," said Dr. Fuddle, "to the crux of the matter." He picked up several pieces of sheet music. "Who'd like to try first?"

"I would," Tyler said, lifting his horn.

"Good," said Dr. Fuddle, opening pieces of music and arranging them onto his stand. "Now I want you to perform the first eight bars of this Bach Minuet. It's not surprising that counterpoint, the presentation of a melody along with its counter melody, is by far the most effective method of controlling a Seiren and renders the ones we've tested incapable of violence."

Einstein pointed Kathy and Tyler in the direction of Seirens numbers One and Two. "Kathy, you'll play the top voice, the upper part, with your viola and Tyler will play the bottom voice. Everyone watch and learn."

Dr. Fuddle instructed Antonio to beat a measure of three counts in preparation and they began to play. By the third measure both creatures were purring.

"Now it's time to bring out one of the fiercest examples of counterpoint ever conceived," Dr. Fuddle said, placing another musical score onto the stands. "This is called the *Grosse Fugue* by Beethoven from his *String Quartet in B-flat Major*."

"Brace yourselves," Einstein said.

Dr. Fuddle motioned for Kathy to play her viola and Leonard his cello. Then he brought forward two other string players, with violins to join them.

The moment Christina stepped forward to watch, the creatures began to shriek.

"Ready?" Dr. Fuddle said. "Play!"

The opening bars of the music caused mixed reaction in the beasts. Some looked strangely contented by the sounds while others turned their backs and tried to cover their diamond-shaped ears. But after a long musical rest, violinist number one pounced into the top voice of the fugue and the beasts clawed at their cages as though they were trying to escape. When Kathy's part joined in, all six Seirens were wailing like demons. But by the time the other two parts joined in the demonstration creating the counterpoint, the Seirens had completely lost any sign of savageness. Their wailing even appeared to be in synch with the music.

"Stop," Dr. Fuddle said.

"Whoa!" Antonio yelled, clapping his hands. "That had to be the coolest thing I've ever seen or heard!"

"Really?" Professor Einstein smiled.

"You're not kidding about the power of counterpoint!" Antonio said. "That was *fierce*. You say that was called the grossest fugue?"

"The *Grosse Fugue*," corrected Dr. Fuddle.

"Now I'm telling you, that was awesome sounding! I'd love for my friends back home to get a load of that. Not to mention for them to see the Seiren freaks trying to get in on it."

Kathy grinned at him. "It's nice to see you're finally developing a sense of taste in music."

Einstein and Dr. Fuddle continued demonstrating how to obtain various results through different of pieces of music. At one point Dr. Fuddle had Antonio drumming a syncopated, irregular beat, then a regular beat to show how the Seirens responded to the difference.

By the end of the practice session, Kathy and Leonard had successfully stopped the movement of the Seirens' wings by playing a Couperin *Allemande* dance piece. Tyler learned how to perform all sorts of musical stunts with his horn. With each successful trial run, he gained more confidence.

Dr. Fuddle and Einstein were amused at the expressions on all of the Messengers' faces. Antonio wanted to play musical tricks on the Seirens all day, but eventually their instructors wrapped up the demonstrations.

"I understand that your team has assembled a task force to retrieve Kathy's viola and Leonard's cello, prior to our approaching the enemy grounds," Dr. Fuddle said to Einstein.

"Yes, Dr. Fuddle. We have worked out our strategy and I will share all the details with you before you depart. I know how vital those instruments are to our success."

"Wonderful." Dr. Fuddle turned to the Messengers. "Do you think you've practiced enough to protect yourself in case you are confronted by Seirens as you proceed?"

"Definitely," Antonio said. "If one of those dudes is on the loose we'll just blast a little gross fugue its way."

"Yeah," Tyler said. "That and resolving the scales should take care of them!"

The others also looked confident.

They followed Einstein out of the area and back to the concrete room with the black boxes. He headed directly for a box of the small reed instruments. "Take these flutes for additional protection," he said, handing out the instruments. "As you can see they are made small enough to fit easily into a pocket. Soon every resident of Orphea will possess one of these, to ward off attacks by the weaker Seirens. They can be used very simply to produce musical pitches."

"I'll teach you how to use these flutes as we head toward our final rehearsal destination and explain in detail our plan of action," Dr. Fuddle added. "Christina, you must remain close to your brother and hold on tightly to your flute."

"You were quick learners. You have bright minds and pure hearts. Be on your way without fear," Einstein said as they left the chambers.

Chapter Fifteen

Leonard hadn't said one word since they had emerged from the underground bunker. As they resumed their journey on the path, he lagged behind.

Kathy slowed her pace to have a few private words with him. "What's wrong?" she asked.

"Don't you see what's happened? Our stupidity's created a big snag in the plan."

"We weren't being stupid!" She tried to keep her voice down. "Even Dr. Fuddle said it wasn't our fault. We were tricked. They've already got that task force to get our instruments back."

"But I went against my gut feeling, Kathy. My father *always* tells me hunches are important, that many great discoveries in science started with instinct. I knew we shouldn't have traded instruments. He always told me there's no easy way past challenges. I didn't trust Dr. Fuddle yet and I wanted you to have that jeweled bracelet."

She squeezed his hand. "That was sweet. I went against my better judgment, too." She looked away.

Dr. Fuddle glanced back at them and they quickened their pace.

"Leonard and Kathy," he said. "Don't create undo pressure on yourselves."

"He heard us," Leonard said.

Kathy nodded. "But I'm responsible for the instruments not being here."

"Not entirely." Leonard's voice broke. "Thanks to me, it's harder for everyone. Now Professor Einstein has one more thing to interrupt his important research."

Dr. Fuddle stopped and looked at Leonard. "Young man, sometimes you simply have to learn to trust."

Leonard quickened his pace. *Why can't I just believe like the others?* he thought.

When they came around a large bend in the path, Tyler was the first to spot the mountain. "Look! That peak goes all the way up into the clouds."

"Are we going up *that*?" Antonio asked.

"Most certainly," Dr. Fuddle said.

"Why can't we take our coach?" Kathy asked.

"It's too steep for horses. We're going to Franz Liszt's rehearsal retreat at the top, where our finest composers will teach you your musical roles so you are ready for battle. Now, prepare yourselves to focus on the task ahead. We have to be assured you are rehearsed and understand precisely how this is going to be accomplished."

"I'm ready for anything!" Tyler said.

Leonard looked as though he wanted to feel the enthusiasm.

"Is everyone ready?" Dr. Fuddle asked. "Let's proceed. Christina, think you can make it? You've already trekked farther than most seven-year-olds."

"Of course!" she wrote on her pad for all to see.

"She can ride on my back," Antonio offered.

Christina shook her head and ran ahead smiling.

"Way to go, Chrissie," Tyler said.

Without missing a beat, they continued upward, higher and higher. The houses in the villages below looked like notes. Christina stopped to look, but only Dr. Fuddle knew how deeply she was affected by the sight of Orphea stretched out in ruins.

Near the end of their challenging climb, wisps of misty clouds enveloped them and the magnificent vistas of Orphea disappeared. As they approached the top, the air grew cooler.

They came upon a spot where the sun broke through. "Shall we take a moment to rest?" Dr. Fuddle said, seeing the Messengers were tiring. Everyone settled onto boulders shaped perfectly for sitting. "I brought along our lunch."

Dr. Fuddle distributed the food prepared by Chef Joseph. They indulged heartily in Sammartini Sandwiches, Frescobaldi Fruit Salad and everyone's favorite from the opening banquet, Rossini Rolls.

Tyler and Antonio finished their lunches first. "Would it be all right for me and Antonio go up ahead to practice?" Tyler's eyes were fixed on a higher rock formation close by.

"Yes, since the others aren't through eating yet. But not for long," Dr. Fuddle replied.

Tyler and Antonio carried their instruments up to a large boulder. "Let's do some improvising," Tyler suggested. Within seconds the two created pleasant new music that drifted through the air. Dr. Fuddle watched them, pleased.

Then something caught Tyler's eye. He saw two small figures farther up standing between two boulders. "That looks like Juliet and Elizabeth," he said. Antonio caught sight of them, too.

"Come on, Tyler," Antonio said, taking the lead with his drum tucked under his arm.

"Wait, Tony," Tyler said. "Something doesn't feel right."

He glanced down at Dr. Fuddle, who was talking to the others. "Okay, but just a quick look."

Tyler and Antonio hiked up toward the mouth of a small cave and sure enough, there stood Juliet and Elizabeth, waving to them.

The girls disappeared into the dark with Antonio following. "What are you two doing here?" he called. "Did those Seirens drop you off all the way up here?"

Tyler looked into the darkness of the cave, clutching a rock, sweating profusely, his fear of the dark returning.

"Hurry up, Tyler!" Antonio yelled.

But Tyler could barely muster up the nerve to take one small step into the black cavern. He looked back again at Dr. Fuddle, hearing laughter as he entertained the others with stories. Comforted by their closeness, Tyler entered the cave. Soon he'd stepped far enough inside that he could no longer see Dr. Fuddle, but could still hear his voice and see the light at the opening of the cave. He took a whiff of the dank, cold air and suddenly felt chilled to the bone. He could barely see Antonio in the dark, and even though Juliet and Elizabeth had disappeared into the blackness, something moved in the shadows.

"Where'd they go?" Antonio whispered, stepping toward Tyler.

"I don't see anybody, but I saw something move. We'd better get out of here fast," Tyler said.

"But what about the girls? We can't leave them here. What if they're in trouble?"

Antonio sat his drum on the ground and trudged several feet farther into the cave. Tyler reluctantly followed him, holding on tightly to his horn.

Behind them it suddenly became dark. They turned to look. The terror of the sight took their breath away. Two great Seirens stood within feet of them, blocking the light from the entrance. The creatures stood staring at them, their cat eyes glaring, narrowed to slits.

"Looking for someone?" Amathes hissed. It raised a wing toward Antonio.

Aplestos, the second Seiren, snarled ferociously, then looked at Amathes, "Shall we?"

"Why not!" Amathes answered. Then, Zap! They changed forms into Elizabeth and Juliet. Then zap! back into their Seiren selves, cackling wildly.

Tyler and Antonio stared with wide-open eyes.

"Holy Mother of God!" Antonio whispered. "Oh, man, Tyler, I'm sorry."

"You and me both," Tyler replied.

"Haven't you ever heard, 'Curiosity killed the cat?'" Aplestos said.

"In this case, the boys?" Amathes amended.

"Should we slay them now?" Aplestos said, crouching down into her feline pounce position. Her tail twitched in anticipation. Tyler and Antonio backed up slowly.

Amathes crouched and whispered in Aplestos' ear. "We can't take the goods by force, remember?"

Tyler lifted the horn to his mouth.

"Put that down!" Aplestos ordered.

Antonio pulled the flute from his pocket.

Aplestos lunged toward Tyler, knocking his horn through the air while Amathes flared his bony wing across Antonio's hand, knocking his flute back into the cave, out of reach.

Tyler grabbed the Seiren's wing, yanking, pulling, twisting it while it shrieked and flapped. "Find your flute!" Tyler yelled to Antonio, hanging on to Aplestos' wing, gouging it with his fingernails.

"Let go!" she screamed. She smashed her wing against the stone wall, nearly crushing Tyler.

Antonio managed to get to his flute. He took a quick breath. "Tyler! I can't remember what to do!"

"Resolve a scale! Resolve a scale!" Tyler screamed, clawing Aplestos' wing until blood gushed out of it.

Antonio raised his flute and shot a full scale into the confines of the cave, stopping on the seventh note then blasting the eighth. The sounds bounced off the rock walls, echoing deep into the cave, reverberating through the bodies of the Seirens until they backed away. With a crazed roar and a powerful swipe, Amathes knocked Tyler off Aplestos' wing, sending him through the air, knocking Antonio to the ground. Antonio regained his footing, and grabbed the drum, but by that time Aplestos had Tyler cornered with her paws around this throat, her open jaw poised over Tyler's head.

"Let my friend go and I'll give you my drum!" Antonio yelled.

"No! Tony! We can't do that! There's got to be another way!"

In a flash, Antonio slipped around Amathes, shoving his drum at Aplestos, who let go of Tyler to grab it. Tyler snatched up his horn and they both scrambled out of the cave, the Seirens screaming in pursuit.

"Run, Ty, run!" Antonio yelled.

Kathy saw them and screamed. "Dr. Fuddle! SEIRENS!" The whole group jumped up yelling and ran toward the boys.

The Seirens flew up into the air and then swooped down over Tyler.

"Let's be off!" Amathes said. "We've got the drum."

The boys collapsed, covered with dirt and blood. Their friends ran to them with Dr. Fuddle close behind.

"They got the drum!" Tyler panted, barely able to catch his breath.

"But Tyler saved his horn!"

"Tony was so brave," Tyler said.

"It all happened so fast! We thought we saw Juliet and Elizabeth in the cave."

"You're hurt!" Kathy exclaimed, running to Tyler.

"Yeah, but not dead," Antonio said.

Christina ran to her brother. She hugged him, blood and all.

"What's the matter with you guys? You should've learned from our experience! We warned you to be on guard!" Leonard shouted.

"I didn't yell at you when you lost your cello, did I?" Antonio replied. "We could've been killed back there. But you just fell for a stupid trick!"

"You shouldn't even have been out of the rooms that night anyway," Tyler said, turning beet red in the face.

"You're right. Sorry." Leonard said, backing off. "But you fell for a stupid trick, too," he mumbled under his breath.

"Save your energy for defeating our enemies," Dr. Fuddle cautioned. They nodded, though both boys were still angry with Leonard. "Losing that drum may well cost us the battle. We must pick up and get to the rehearsal hall immediately. It's urgent our head composers know what's happened."

Though Dr. Fuddle showed no ill temper, his words cut right into Tyler's heart. How could he have let this happen? How could there be anything inside of him that could lead them to victory?

Dr. Fuddle played a short, haunting melody on his lyre causing Tyler and Antonio's cuts to instantly stop bleeding. The friends stared in awe. Their wounds were completely healed.

Chapter Sixteen

May it not be too late, Dr. Fuddle prayed silently. He led the group through a narrow rocky pass until they arrived at Liszt's lakeside mountain retreat that had been enlarged to include space for rehearsals.

Sadness overwhelmed them as they neared the retreat. The devastation was horrendous. With few trees left unscathed, only traces of the last natural beauty of Orphea remained. Christina leaned over to smell a withered pink flower on a bush lining a crumbled walkway, but none of the fragrance remained.

Dr. Fuddle approached the front door as it opened.

"Come in," a tall, handsome man said. He greeted Dr. Fuddle with a firm handshake, but underneath his charm lurked the grim understanding of the urgency of the times. The stress of the continual Seiren attacks seemed to have weakened his dazzling smile.

Dr. Fuddle introduced the Messengers, then said: "This man standing before you is none other than Franz Liszt—the greatest pianist of all time."

Liszt bowed humbly. "It's wonderful to meet you at last. I

have some good news. We know the whereabouts of the stolen instruments."

"You do?" Tyler asked. "Even the drum?"

"Yes. I've already communicated with our spies."

Dr. Fuddle looked very pleased.

"And they know their exact location."

"Where are they?" Leonard asked.

"On the grounds of the enemy fortress, far into Dis."

"Excellent!" Tyler exclaimed.

"Yes." Dr. Fuddle responded. "However, Jedermann knows the power the instruments possess. He knows the only way of stopping that power is to destroy all of them completely."

Tyler held tightly to his horn.

Kathy panicked. "This is horrible! Normally I'm much more trustworthy when I'm given something valuable. But the impersonators were so persuasive..." her voice trailed off.

"We don't have time to worry, only to act. We must move quickly," Liszt said. "The timing of this is crucial. We must get those instruments back into your hands before we invade."

"I know we will get them back," Tyler said with conviction.

Kathy agreed. "I *must* make up for my mistake."

"No question!" Antonio said.

"Good," Liszt replied. He led the way into the large rehearsal hall overlooking an immense valley, surrounded by jagged, steep cliffs. Dr. Fuddle briefly looked into the valley and shook his head at the terrible destruction, which had over-taken this once awe-inspiring view.

A piano stood in the center of the large room with glass-paned doors that overlooked an outdoor terrace. An adjacent hallway led to several other rooms.

"This is where I practice," Liszt said. He walked toward the piano, gazing out the glass doors and noticed that gloom seemed to seep through the valley.

Dr. Fuddle pointed to a piece of music laid out above the keyboard. "Take a look at this music," he said, while they gathered around.

Kathy looked at the musical score with interest. "Do you think I could ever play that?"

"If you worked hard enough, Kathy," Liszt said. "I had to practice fourteen to sixteen hours a day to master it."

"Fourteen to sixteen hours a day?"

"Yes," he replied. "But I was so inspired it didn't seem like work."

Liszt looked longingly out into the valley. "Nothing is more important than inspiration, especially now. When I was just a young man I went to a concert that inspired me for life. Everyone in Europe raved about this violinist named Paganini taking the concert halls by storm. One day I went to hear him."

Kathy listened, fascinated.

"I tell you, his performance was a spectacle like I'd never seen. He performed with the passion of a madman—the bow bounced off the strings as they broke one by one. Magnificent music roared through the air." Liszt raised his right fist. "Afterwards, I vowed to myself: What this man has done for the violin, I shall do for the piano!"

Dr. Fuddle kept a watchful eye on the valley below. "Soon we must put our plan into action, but first we offer you final inspiration before your work begins."

Liszt seated himself at the piano. "Allow me. Jedermann may have stolen the Gold Baton, our lightning rod of inspiration, but he can't steal what we have in our hearts. I have some special guests here to help me. Come forward, my little friends!"

A group of gnomes rushed into the room. They bowed dramatically before the Messengers. Each one was short and stout with a smiling face and round, rosy cheeks.

Christina, in particular, enjoyed the frolicking characters while Dr. Fuddle threw open the glass doors to let the mountain air fill the room.

"What I'll play for you today is called *Gnomenreigen*, 'Dance of the Gnomes.'"

"It's so difficult, most people thought it was impossible to play," Dr. Fuddle said.

Christina sat on the floor, inviting the others to do the same. The gnomes assumed their postures, with the head gnome, Erkenbald, taking the lead.

"Dance my friends—dance your hearts out!" Liszt raised his hands high above the keys and closed his eyes.

"Release your imaginations!" Dr. Fuddle said to his pupils, but tears filled his eyes as he thought: *May this not be the last time you witness the power of great music!*

Liszt's long fingers pounced upon the piano keyboard. Magical sounds showered the listeners. His fingers raced with swift ease as his blurred hands crisscrossed in and out of the black and white keys. Such passion for music none of them had ever seen.

Surely his fingers, hands, and arms will become entangled! Kathy thought.

Dr. Fuddle smiled. He welcomed the relief the music brought from the terrors happening across Orphea. When the music increased its fury, the gnomes winked at one another, plunging into the wildest dance ever seen. On and on the music and movement whirled until the gnomes grabbed Christina and Tyler by the arms, pulling them into the dance and out onto the terrace. The others, enchanted by the spell, joined in.

But then, off in the distance, beyond the glories of the music, came the threatening sound of wings. Jedermann could not possibly let such an opportunity pass. He lay in wait for any chance to disrupt the grandeur of the Orpheans' beautiful moments. It was not yet the time for Jedermann to confront his nemesis, Dr. Fuddle, so he sent his lowly Seirens, who could scarcely contain themselves at the prospect of such shameful fun. They flew in their monstrous pack—hundreds of them in number—toward the musical festivities. They clutched in their paws filthy little packages—plant bombs from the bogs—and they hissed in glee, anticipating pelting their loathsome litter onto the happy faces of the Messengers, replacing the music with havoc.

The appalling pack of Seirens approached from the air, unnoticed by Liszt and his enthralled dancers. The villainous pack flew over, flinging their putrid pellets, which plunged toward the Messengers. Suddenly plant bombs were exploding around them.

"Don't let fear win!" Dr. Fuddle urged. "Confront it with the joy of music!" With these words they danced with rekindled hope, dancing more excitedly than ever.

Dr. Fuddle strummed his lyre. He closed his eyes, envisioning sacred beauty—envisioning the look of enchantment in the eyes of the Messengers—listening only to the harmonies of the powerful music. Magically, Dr. Fuddle's musical notes formed into bubbles in the air, transforming the filth into splendor. The exploding barrage of trash from the enemy invaders changed, in a powerful flash of great light, into millions of white rose petals, which fluttered onto the dancers. The scent of the perfumed snow-like petals blew like a cloud into the air, scattering the airborne beasts away from Liszt's retreat and back to Dis.

With an other-worldly expression, Dr. Fuddle observed the happiness of the friends. The joy he felt in his heart made him feel as though he were floating high above all of them. And then, with one final flurry across the keys, Liszt finished the piece, mesmerizing one and all with the magic of his performance. For a moment no one moved or spoke.

Tyler wiped the sweat off his forehead.

Christina felt as though her feet would never touch the ground again, so happy was she with the music and dancing and being covered in the velvety white rose petals.

"Liszt performed like this all over Europe, I tell you!" Dr. Fuddle exclaimed. "He was the biggest star of them all! And we, the people of Orphea *will* reclaim the stars, every last one of them!"

Liszt stood from the piano. A look of humility danced across his handsome face. He gazed out the window, trying to focus on his memories of untouched beauty.

"The mountains and the lakes," he said, "they were my rewards." He glanced at Dr. Fuddle with admiration, then turned to the Messengers: "I am filled with gratitude that a Great Spirit such as your mentor here, Benjamin Fuddle, would arise and dedicate his soul to our sacred Art—to carry it to beings across the universe."

Kathy, moved by this tribute, ran to embrace both Liszt and Dr. Fuddle, holding back no longer, revealing the delight this music evoked deep within her. The others couldn't believe their eyes at her uncharacteristic display.

"Oh, how you've inspired me!" she said to Liszt, wiping tears from her eyes. It was at this exact moment that she knew: "I want to play this music more than anything I've ever wanted in my whole life. I'll practice every spare moment. This is what I want to do—what I must do—for the rest of my life."

Dr. Fuddle was so moved by her newfound enthusiasm a lump grew in his throat.

With this, Liszt stepped toward her and kissed her on the forehead, remembering vividly the time he was eleven years old and had met Beethoven, who'd kissed his forehead and spoken immortal words to him. "I shall look forward to great things from you, my dear."

But Dr. Fuddle knew the time had come to face the inevitable. He took on a serious expression as he turned to the gnomes. "Now, our helpers," he said, "you must go forward into the enemy territory while we prepare. Report to us the latest activities of the Seirens and find ways to distract them, to conceal our coming."

They bowed to Dr. Fuddle and the Messengers and scurried out.

"All right, honored Messengers of Music, gather around," Liszt said. "It is time to make our final preparations." He gathered a large pile of music from a table nearby and distributed it. "Czerny will teach you the importance of form and structure, Mozart will teach you lyricism—the fine art of performing in a song-like manner, I will hone your technique, Prokofiev will drill your rhythms and Rachmaninoff will demonstrate bravura performance style—performing with brilliance! Dr. Fuddle will oversee the entire process."

"We will use this as our master classroom for your basic instructions," Dr. Fuddle explained. "You must learn your parts flawlessly, regardless of the instrument you play. It has been scientifically proven that this musical work can bring down our enemy."

"The leaders of Orphea have voted unanimously on the music to be used," Liszt continued. "It is the *Finale* of Sergei Rachmaninoff's *Third Concerto for the Piano*. It's scored for woodwinds, brass and percussion sections, plus full strings including string bass."

"Without a doubt," Dr. Fuddle added, "This masterwork has the exact combinations of instruments, rhythms, notes and their timbres or tonal qualities, to produce the ultimate vibrations to not only paralyze Jedermann *but to transform his entire army*." He paused then instructed, "We will now drill you on your parts until you thoroughly memorize them."

"Even as we speak, our reinforcements—the people of our fair Orphea—armed with the specially designed flutes," Liszt added, "are marching to surround the enemy grounds, to back us as we storm Jedermann's fortress. Our top musicians have learned their parts, and are prepared for battle."

"And we've been given the ultimate task of preparing you," Dr. Fuddle said. "For you, the destined Messengers of Music, will lead us. According to the prophecy, you will head our orchestral army to reclaim what belongs to us: our children and the Gold Baton!"

"How do you know for sure this will work?" Leonard asked.

Dr. Fuddle looked at Liszt, then the others, taking his time before answering.

Tyler stared at Dr. Fuddle. A remarkable bond had bloomed between them, blossoming more fully than the millions of flowers that had once graced Orphea. Tyler felt somehow he'd always known him. His attachment to his teacher grew stronger by the minute. Only he and his sister realized the extent of great sorrow brooding beneath Dr. Fuddle's courageous face. They knew his words would be memorable, just like the words of their mother when she talked about music.

"While we know the science behind the sound," Dr. Fuddle said with an all-knowing smile, "we also know the ultimate truth: Mediocrity cannot survive the shining light of Excellence."

The friends digested his words and prepared their instruments and musical scores while the composers and musicians filed in to arrange themselves around them.

They practiced their parts repeatedly until their hands

cramped in pain, until everyone could play with greater accuracy.

"Do you think we can ever get this right?" Antonio complained.

"Yes, but it may take hundreds of more attempts," Dr. Fuddle said. "Keep working hard."

At one point, Tyler's French horn part became so difficult Mozart had him sing the melody one hundred times in a row until it sounded perfectly lyrical.

"I think I've got it now," Tyler said. He could feel the music becoming a part of his soul.

Kathy and Leonard had to work equally hard memorizing their lines, especially at the very ending with all its difficult leaps and double stops. "We're getting it, Leonard, we're getting these notes!" Kathy said, beaming.

"You're right—I feel it coming—let's just keep going until *it is flawless*," he replied.

After the rehearsals finally finished, everyone knew their parts backward and forward. They felt energized and determined like never before.

"Jedermann knows we're coming," Dr. Fuddle warned. "He'll stop at nothing to try to prevent us from moving ahead. He'll do anything to destroy goodness. His very survival depends upon trying to stop the eternal seeds of greatness—not only in all that is visible, but in the invisible hearts and minds of every living being."

"Soon you shall see the extent of his wicked power," Liszt continued. "But now you are prepared to face him and his Seiren army. You're now armed to go into his evil domain. We pray that we possess the power to bring him down—hopefully once and for all."

Dr. Fuddle turned first to Tyler.

"Are *you* ready?"

Although Tyler couldn't imagine exactly what lay ahead, he knew he was ready. The scene of leading his friends through the open door of Dr. Fuddle's mansion—at what seemed like a lifetime earlier—flashed through his mind.

"Yes," he said. "This is it! What do you say everyone?"

He offered his hand to his friends to form a sacred pact. Never in his life had he felt such courage.

Antonio placed his hand on Tyler's. "I'm in."

"I knew I could count on you. I've always known it," Tyler said.

Leonard's hand followed. "I'm with you every step of the way."

Then Kathy's. "You can count on me. Now *this* is what I call important."

"Christina?" Tyler asked, looking into his sister's eyes.

With a look of fearless courage, she placed her tiny hand above her brother's in the solemn pact. She then placed Dolly face down above their hands and pulled the tattered string, which enabled her doll to talk. "Hello, I'm Dolly," it said. Everyone laughed.

"Dolly's in!" Antonio declared.

Dr. Fuddle smiled. He then placed his left hand under Tyler's and his right hand over the doll with Christina's hand below. They looked into one another's eyes while the composers watched in admiration.

Then Tyler said, "Now, let's go make history!"

Chapter Seventeen

Before leaving Liszt's retreat, the Messengers of Music welcomed the farewell hugs of the demanding composers who had trained them. After they said their final goodbyes they marched back onto the path toward Dis with Dr. Fuddle at their side.

From time to time, they looked back at Orphea's highest mountain with Liszt's retreat fading into the distance. They'd entered their musical training with fear but had finished as brave soldiers. Music was now a part of their being and they possessed a new respect for the musical giants who came before them. They also had renewed respect for each other.

Threatening clouds gathered over the mountains of Dis, darkening the sky, as if warning that trouble lay ahead—that victory would not come easily. They held their instruments bravely.

"Remain calm at what we now shall see," Dr. Fuddle said.

They reached the brow of the mountain and stopped at an overlook. A sight so shocking met their eyes they could not speak. Starless twilight suffocated the peaks of the mountain-tops as far as they could see. Meadows once green lay parched and barren, forests burned, lakes putrefied with decay. Bridges jutted at odd angles, most of them destroyed and impassable. Dread flooded over Tyler, Christina and their friends, who moved closer together, feeling vulnerable in this great wasteland without the grand structures and positive energies of Orphea to protect them.

"Look," Tyler pointed out, "you can still see the main path. It's unbroken and leads to that largest bridge and far beyond." His words were little comfort. The path looked like a thin thread overpowered by the bleak surroundings, winding into nothingness.

"Yes, unbroken," said their mentor, "because it is like a scarlet thread of hope, never wavering, never changing, always there to show you the way."

Their eyes followed a towering peak that rose above all the others, out of the mist.

Kathy gripped Leonard's arm. "Do you see that?" she whispered.

"That must be Jedermann's fortress," he answered.

Dr. Fuddle nodded. "That's right. Our destination."

Everyone shuddered at the thought. Dark and menacing, it looked evil, like a fortress of death, with five tremendous towers rising into the sky, in a pentagram arrangement.

It took all of Kathy's inner strength to even look at what lay before them. "They've turned this heaven into hell," she said.

"Yes, that's true, I'm afraid," Dr. Fuddle said. "But don't forget heaven reigns wherever there is harmony. Darkness reigns wherever cacophony prevails. We must proceed. Come, my brave Messengers."

Dr. Fuddle guided them along the winding path. They held hands, picking their way slowly, as they maneuvered along a steep cliff. They stopped at the edge and stared at the damaged stone bridge spanning the deep gorge.

"Don't tell me we have to go across that!" Leonard said. "It doesn't look too safe."

"I'm afraid we must go across," Dr. Fuddle said. "It's the only way we can get into Dis from here." He led them carefully onto the bridge. They couldn't bear to look over the edges, far down to the river. Tyler's heart pounded as they huddled closely together. It was the first time he'd thought of counting for a long time.

Halfway across, Christina heard a strange noise, like a fluttering sound. She released her brother's hand and stopped for a moment, looking behind her. Then she heard it again. But this time it was accompanied by soft footsteps on the bridge quite a distance back. She stopped once more, turning her head to look. To her surprise there stood two pretty little girls singing a tune that only she could hear. They stepped out of a mysterious wisp of cloud and beckoned for her to join them. Christina lagged behind the others to stare at the girls, who waved to her. The urge to play with them overpowered her and she walked toward them.

At the same time Kathy pointed to a white egret that had landed on the stone post farther along the bridge. "Such a beautiful sight in the midst of all the decay."

Dr. Fuddle and the others approached the bird quietly, so as not to scare it away. Tyler was entranced and didn't even notice Christina wasn't at his side. He had never seen a bird like this in the wild.

Meanwhile, Christina walked closer to the girls. Her mind felt as hazy as the unusual cloud with each step she took. She heard strange words in another language. They sounded very sweet, but unfamiliar.

"Du liebest Kind, komm geh mit mir," one of the little girls uttered in a mystifying whisper.

Enticing, pleasant, rang these words and somehow the

meaning seemed clear. *Lovely child, come go with me.* They were beautiful, friendly girls. One of them looked like little Regina Bach, who gave Tyler the horn. How pleasant it might be to meet them, she thought. All she had to do was let Tyler and Dr. Fuddle know what she was doing, but the girls' alluring power strengthened and she couldn't turn around. Instead, she watched the fog curl around their tiny golden slippers as she walked toward them.

"Gar schöne spiele spiel' ich mit dir," the other whispered to Christina while she approached. Christina somehow knew they'd said *many lovely games I'll play with you.*

Christina could see the girls were friendly, probably from a nearby village. She thought it wouldn't be necessary to get anyone's attention—that Tyler and Dr. Fuddle would soon turn around and see the girls, too. Dr. Fuddle rarely missed anything. He'd allow one last pleasant time for play before the battle. They needed that little bit of lightness and fun.

"Manch' bunte Blumen sind am dem Strand,
Meine Mutter hat manch gulden Gewand!"

This time the words came from an unseen fatherly voice, behind the girls, which sounded like Bach's voice. Christina thought he'd said *many colorful flowers are on the shore. My mother has many golden robes.* He must have known how Christina adored flowers and how she loved her mother's golden garments.

The girls offered Christina some colorful flowers, but strangely, the flowers and the girls began to disappear into the mist. The odd little tune coming from behind the girls grew a little louder. She hurried toward the girls, hoping to reach them to accept the flowers before they were gone.

Just when she reached for their beautiful bouquet, the little girls snatched it away and suddenly transformed into their true horrifying forms of Aplestos and Amathes who stood sneering at her. They grabbed her wrists. She wanted to scream but could-n't, of course, and clung tightly to Dolly. The once enchanting mist choked her. The Seirens twisted her wrists, dragging her more deeply into the cloud. Suddenly she stood before a being so frightening, she barely remained conscious. No longer could she hear Dr. Fuddle's voice or the others. The monster loomed over her, twitching his ugly black-veined wings.

Somehow she knew it was Jedermann.

"Is this what everyone's looking for, little girl?!" he snarled. He held high in the air what looked like a stick that had burned black as coal. He waved it closer to her, with a frightening gleam in his eyes.

"Neither Dr. Fuddle nor anyone in Orphea will ever get this baton back!" he hissed, spraying her with his spit, with-drawing it with a snap. "Ever!"

"Why are you listening to Dr. Fuddle anyway?" Amathes asked.

"He knows nothing. You shouldn't have trusted him," Aplestos scolded.

Jedermann took a small step back, spreading his wings, leering at her innocent face. "What makes anyone listen to him?" he demanded. He paused and waited for her response. "Well?" He lunged toward her, jutting his scarred face within inches of hers. "Answer me, you little fool!" he huffed. His putrid breath almost gagged her. "Answer me now!"

Christina struggled against her captors, but it was no use, her physical strength was feeble compared to theirs. Knowing her weakness, they released her right wrist and took a long look at her.

"What's wrong with you, girl?" Amathes mocked.

"Cat got your tongue?" Aplestos cackled. Christina strug-gled against the grip of another saber-toothed Seiren that had emerged from beneath the bridge.

DR. FUDDLE AND THE GOLD BATON

Jedermann looked at Christina carefully. "What is wrong with you?" he demanded. He glared at her. "Answer me, I say!"

Christina felt disoriented but not doomed. She somehow believed deep inside that her brother and Dr. Fuddle wouldn't let anything happen to her.

"You can't talk, can you?" Jedermann scorned. He laughed cruelly. "You pitiful little child!"

His Seiren captains joined in the laughter. Jedermann raised his arm to strike her, as if to cast her down, down, down into the gorge below just to scare her. Two other lowly Seirens foamed at their mouths, cheering her helplessness. They grabbed her with their long sinewy paws, handing her over to Jedermann.

Tyler heard their treacherous laughter and yelled, *"WHERE'S CHRISTINA?"*

The friends all turned around in horror to stare through the mist to witness her terrifying situation.

Dr. Fuddle strummed his lyre with one stroke, instantly transporting all of them to her side. They landed in front of Jedermann, who smiled with fiendish pleasure.

"You let go of my sister!" Tyler yelled.

Antonio and Leonard started to jump at the enemies but Dr. Fuddle held them back. He motioned for all of them to get behind him, never taking his gaze off Jedermann.

Amathes and Aplestos snarled, ready to pounce, but Jedermann signaled for them to be quiet, glaring into his arch-enemy's eyes. The air crackled with the power of the two opponents meeting face to face for the first time in ages. Dr. Fuddle glared back with a fierceness none of the Messengers could've dreamed possible.

"So, we meet again, Jedermann, after all this time."

Jedermann loosened his grip on Christina. "I've got some good news Dr. Fuddle, want to hear?"

"I have no interest in what you have to say, Jedermann. You might have been the best had you not chosen the easier path. Release her—NOW!"

"Don't be so demanding," he jeered, raising Christina by one arm over the railing of the bridge. They all gasped. "It seems I have a little more advantage at the moment." He smirked at Dr. Fuddle. "Well, old man, you will *never* win against the great Jedermann again! You beat me in the most important event of my career. I was banished from Orphea because of you. You claimed victory once over me, but since I couldn't claim the title of the best musician in Orphea, I vowed no one would have music! No one!"

"Your failure was *not* because of me, Jedermann," Dr. Fuddle said with dignity. "It was your philosophy of just 'getting by' that doomed you to mediocrity. You coasted on your appearance and talent. You were never committed to excellence."

"Outrage!" Jedermann cried. "But now look what I have for my prize!" He clutched Christina firmly and with his other hand swept the black scepter, no longer recognizable, from beneath his cloak. "And you will never solve the mystery of how I took ownership of your precious baton."

Dr. Fuddle moved boldly toward Jedermann. With several powerful strums of his lyre half of the Seirens fell headfirst off the bridge, screeching all the way down, their wings failing.

"No, no, no. Not another move or this little girl dies!" Jedermann shouted.

"You will never get away with this," Dr. Fuddle shouted.

"No? You really think you have the power to stop me? Oh, I think not!"

He smirked at Tyler, "On second thought, maybe I'll permit you to play a little 'over the bridge lullaby' for your baby sister. How's that sound, you sissy? And what about you, Prissy," his dark gaze fell on Kathy, "you want to play the little fiddle for your friend one last time?"

Kathy glared at him in disgust.

"I'd like to play a lullaby, as a matter of fact," Tyler said, taking his French horn out of its case and putting the mouth-piece to his lips.

"You play one note and your little speechless sister dies!" Jedermann held Christina out even farther over the bridge.

"NO!" Antonio screamed.

"Oh, what a shame, *children*," Jedermann mocked. He looked at their terrified faces. "You've managed to make it this far, but it seems I have three of your real...what are they called again?...the *sacred* instruments of Orpheus?"

Dr. Fuddle's eyes blazed. He raised his arm ready to use his powers by force once more.

"Now, now, now, Dr. Fuddle—I'm warning you! Besides, that won't be necessary," Jedermann said. "Here's the deal I have for you. It's very simple."

"Hand her over! NOW!" Dr. Fuddle ordered.

Jedermann twisted Christina's arm. Tyler grew red with rage.

"Stop babbling, Fuddle," Jedermann frothed. "I'll hand her back when you agree to my terms."

"You hand her over now, you freak!" Antonio yelled. He started to race toward Jedermann, but was stopped by Dr. Fuddle's arm.

"Stop being so testy, pretty boy," Jedermann said. He looked Christina over. "Now, clearly I have no use for this lit-tle girl."

Tyler fumed. He feared he'd pass out from anger.

"But this," he said, holding the blackened baton with his free hand, "I've had plenty of use for. Soon everyone in Orphea will be won over to my way of doing things." He smiled at the scepter.

"I may even decide to remodel all of Orphea like Dis, once I'm in full control," Jedermann said. "Fuddle, you should've known I'd have the power to stop your half-baked scheme to train these 'Messes of Music' to reclaim power. Surely you didn't underestimate me that much, did you, Dr. Fuddie Duddie? Do you really think the Prophecy of Orpheus is the last word around here?"

Dr. Fuddle held his tongue.

"So here's the deal," Jedermann continued. He lowered Christina back onto the bridge. She slumped to the ground. Dr. Fuddle sent her loving waves of energy to sustain her. "If you take these kids out of here and vow never to return, I'll give her back unharmed. Just use your magic and return to the Golden Doors. I'll lock them behind you for good. It's that simple. Orphea will be mine forever."

Dr. Fuddle remained silent.

"Can't you see that your plan was useless? It's too late. Don't you understand? Orphea is already mine and everyone in it. Did you really think you could stop me after all the progress I've made? You and those wigged weirdos and these pathetic excuses for musicians?"

"You'll NEVER win against Dr. Fuddle!" Antonio shouted.

"Or against the other great men who rule Orphea!" Leonard said.

"You're nothing but a detestable piece of filth!" Kathy yelled. She started to spit at him but Leonard held her back.

"Silence! All of you!" Jedermann yelled. "Fuddle and I have some unfinished business." He turned back to his enemy. "Well? What's your decision?"

Dr. Fuddle gazed with fiery intensity into Jedermann's black eyes. "On my word, Jedermann, hand Christina over safely and we'll be gone."

Tyler believed Dr. Fuddle had just sold his own soul to save Christina's life.

"One false move, Fuddle, and they all die," Jedermann

warned. He released Christina. She ran into the arms of Dr. Fuddle, who gave her over to Tyler. She held Dolly tightly while Tyler gave her a long hug.

Dr. Fuddle stared at Jedermann. "You may think you've won this battle, Jedermann, but you haven't won ..."

Before he could finish his sentence, Jedermann whipped the blackened baton through the air, unleashing an entire flock of saber-toothed Seirens from beneath the bridge. In a barrage of utter chaos, the Seirens grabbed all the instruments and surrounded Tyler, Christina and Dr. Fuddle.

"All rules are off now!" Jedermann howled.

The saber-toothed Seirens chanted their hisses while the other Seirens screeched. Their cacophonous wails were so excruciating Christina could hardly bear it. Tyler tried to shield her ears.

Dr. Fuddle reached for his lyre, but before he could strum a single tone Jedermann swiped it from him with his powerful wing, knocking it down into the gorge.

"Protect yourself now, oh, Great Fuddle!" Jedermann roared. His hideous laughter rang off the steep cliffs.

Antonio, Leonard and Kathy screamed for their friends and Dr. Fuddle, who were fighting their way in vain through the pack of hissing and viciously clawing Seirens that surrounded them. But right before their terrified eyes, the Seirens' dissonant shrieks turned Dr. Fuddle a deathly white. He tried to lift his arm but it failed him. He tried to move his legs, but they'd turned to stone.

Jedermann raised the baton and howled, reveling in the sight of his helpless arch nemesis. Dr. Fuddle's eyes remained focused on him until the harsh tones turned them to ice.

Tyler reached for Dr. Fuddle, hoping his touch could restore him, but it was too late. The relentless unleashing of disharmony caused his teacher's hands to crack, turning them into a chalky snow blowing into the wind. Soon his entire body cracked and turned to white dust.

In horror, the Messengers watched the last remnants of their beloved mentor disintegrate until he disappeared completely. He was gone. Only his voice lingered, but just for a brief moment.

"Trust your hearts," the voice said.

A moment of deathly silence prevailed.

"Fools!" Jedermann howled. He raised himself into the air and beat his wings with a deafening roar, looking down at Dr. Fuddle's ashes. "I've beaten you, at last!"

Suddenly a Seiren swooped in and snatched Christina. It teased Tyler, flying almost within his reach, gripping his little sister tightly and snarling. His heart nearly burst as he jumped up, trying to reach her.

With a final shriek the Seirens took off, flying behind their master toward his domain.

Just before Jedermann was out of sight he turned and yelled, "Good luck trying to get home. You'll never make it!"

Christina and Dolly, dangling in the air, disappeared with the brutal mob of Seirens as they flew off into the distance.

Chapter Eighteen

The four remaining figures appeared as tiny specks in the monstrous field of devastation. The heavens wept. The scorched spruces and firs wailed in the wind; the musical leaves of the oaks, birches, aspens, and elms fell to the ground, a withered crackling brown. The yellow asters, purple violets and white honeysuckle wept, wilted and died. The rivers and streams stopped flowing. The red cardinals, meadowlarks, mountain bluebirds, and golden warblers fluttered around the young people, but their songs were silenced and their colors faded.

Antonio staggered, dazed from the intensity of the fighting and his bleeding wounds.

Kathy, in shock, paced frantically back and forth at the scene of terror. "I can't believe this. I just can't believe it."

Leonard was crushed. Just when he trusted like the others, his newfound faith was wrenched away from him. He stalked up to Tyler. "How could this have happened? This wasn't supposed to happen! I thought we were destined to win!"

Tyler stood shaking, aching from the devastating loss of Christina and Dr. Fuddle. He took in a deep breath of air and suddenly felt filled with light. His face looked radiant, his hair shined. He felt profound compassion for his friends. "I don't know what's next," he confessed. "But we haven't come this far for nothing. I *do know* we are the Messengers of Music sent to deliver Orphea. I know my mother is with us—somehow, someway. With everything that's happened—everything we've seen, we can't doubt ourselves now. You heard Dr. Fuddle's last words. Trusting will get us to where we need to go. I wouldn't blame you if you wanted to go back home, but I'll save Christina and Orphea if I have to do it single-handedly."

The confidence in his voice brought a ray of hope to everyone.

"Some deliverers we are," Antonio said. "We were powerless against those monsters."

For a moment no one said anything else.

Then Leonard broke the silence. "We can still be the defenders of Orphea."

Antonio and Kathy looked at him, astonished. For some reason the tone of Leonard's voice didn't surprise Tyler. He believed his friend had enormous inner strength; that he'd turn out to be one of the strong ones.

"Everyone is counting on us." For the first time in Leonard's life, he was taking a step of blind faith. "And we'll get back home somehow, too."

"You're right," Tyler said. "We are the deliverers. I knew the moment I heard that music from Dr. Fuddle's house—I knew that very night was the beginning of a new path for me. And I knew the moment I saw Dr. Fuddle he had to be the great teacher my mother told me about. This can't be the end. We have to carry on, for Christina and for what we promised we'd do."

"I agree, Tyler. We'll figure out a way," Leonard said. His face showed strength and resolve. "And we still have these," he said, producing the small flute out of his pocket. He walked to Kathy and put his arms around her. "I know we'll never see Dr. Fuddle again…" he paused, holding back tears, "…but we'll rescue Christina and do what we're here to do in Dr. Fuddle's honor." The others nodded.

"Besides, we're not alone here," Kathy added, wanting to be supportive, even in the smallest way. "We've still got our whole army of composers and gnomes and the people of Orphea—and maybe even the entranced ones will break free and join us."

Tyler agreed, "You're right, Kathy. Let's just think this through calmly, if we can. He pointed toward Jedermann's castle. "Let's keep moving and trust our hearts." The thought of the possible dangers ahead sent a look of determination across his face.

"I'm not leaving you here, Tyler," Antonio said. Tyler looked gratefully into the eyes of his best friend.

"I'd never leave you either," Leonard said. "We've all got to stay together."

"Maybe we can go back and find help," Kathy said. "We can make it back up the mountain to Liszt and the other composers. They weren't that far back. We have to tell them what's happened. They'll help us. They'll know what to do."

"There's no time to go back," Tyler said. "We have to move forward and do what we're here to do. We must rescue Christina and the army is surely ahead waiting to help us. We can do this. They need us now more than ever. I can feel it. Is everyone with me?"

The four of them looked at one another. Kathy took a step toward Tyler and hugged him. She looked at the castle and nodded. "We're with you Tyler. Let's go."

Tyler led his friends off the bridge, toward the castle. "Come on, then. There's no time to waste. I have no doubt we can protect ourselves with the flutes. Let's just remember everything we've been taught and stick together."

* * * * *

"Fools! Fooo——ellls!" Jedermann screamed, looking into his music box. Amathes and Aplestos stood by his side watching Tyler and his friends head their way toward his citadel.

"Shall we stop them, Master?" Aplestos asked.

"Stop them?" Jedermann replied. "Of course not, I want them here. I want to see if they'll join the others and become our slaves when we take full control of Orphea. I credit Aplestos for that superbly wicked idea." He smiled at her then looked out the windows of his quarters, onto the courtyard below where hundreds of his victims walked about aimlessly. "The more the merrier. And if they don't decide to join us, we'll imprison them in isolated cells like Christina during the burning ceremony, then finish them off once and for all."

"Or better, yet, Master? May I suggest we finish them off by burning them along with the instruments?" Amathes licked his tiger chops. I like my meat well-done."

"Only if persuasion is not possible. You must learn to look beyond mere strength and see the more sophisticated point of view if you ever wish to progress in your career."

Amathes growled and Aplestos smiled for she knew she was the one with the brains.

Jedermann looked back at the images floating out of the music box. "Dr. Fuddle thought those children could take all this away? The people of Orphea thought *those kids* were their saviors?" His words incited a frenzied gale of laughter from the lower Seirens. He again looked out the window down into the courtyard. His drummers pounded off beat without any sense of rhythm. Horrific disharmony filled every corner. There stood in the center the huge stack of wood prepared for the bonfire. In the place of honor to top the pile, lay Leonard's cello, Kathy's viola, Antonio's drum, and now Tyler's French horn—soon to smoke and burn and play no more.

"No one could ever stop you, Master!" Aplestos said.

"You are so absolutely correct, my darling feline. No one has ever been able to stop me where I've made my mark. It will only be a matter of time before everyone in Orphea will bow to me."

Chapter Nineteen

"I can't see the castle any longer," Kathy said.

The sight of Jedermann's looming towers disappeared behind the tall evergreens, but they all sensed they were getting nearer.

"We'll know where to go," Tyler said. "Just keep moving." The Liszt mountain retreat and the bridge were long out of sight. They'd entered an entangled area of forest, with broken limbs and rotted logs scattered in all directions. It grew darker and more stifling with each step.

Antonio stripped off his t-shirt and wiped the sweat off his forehead. "Is it me or is it getting hotter?" Everyone noticed a drastic temperature difference the farther they walked. The air seemed to stagnate, hanging heavily all around them.

"Look!" Tyler pointed off to the left, spotting a strip of bare dirt. "It looks like a trail. Let's take a look." Tyler said.

"Good eye, Tyler," Leonard said.

They stepped off the main path and pushed branches aside to follow the dirt path. The underbrush grew thicker and thicker, but large sections had been ripped away from the trail in places.

"We're not the first to come this way," Tyler said.

They came to a wall of rocks with a sign, obscured by the dense foliage. It was different from all the other signs they'd seen in Orphea. A narrow tunnel-like archway with two closed wooden gates stood at the end. Tangled branches grew in every direction. Tyler and Antonio pulled away a twisted knot of vines. The sign behind it read:

EINGANG ZU VERBOTEN DOMÄNE
UND BIST DU NICHT WILLIG,
SO BRAUCH ICH GEWALT

"What's that mean?" Antonio asked.

"The top line means 'entrance to the forbidden domain,'" Kathy said.

"What's the bottom line mean?" Tyler asked.

She read it and shuddered. "Sure you want to hear? It means 'and if you're not willing, I shall use force,'" she answered. "That's from a famous poem called 'Der Erlkönig.' My grandfather often read it to me."

"Seems clear this is a way in to Jedermann's fortress. Let's go," Tyler said. He looked around before he motioned the others to follow him into the dark archway. The boys rammed their shoulders into the gates that were more than twice their size. They pushed and pushed until they finally creaked open.

On the other side the trail continued, but showed clear signs of earlier struggles. Small trees were pulled leafless, like they'd been held onto for dear life. Leonard pointed to the deep claw marks scuffing the ground everywhere.

They left the open doors behind and walked up the trail, coming to a clearing. With each step the heat became almost unbearable.

Suddenly, Antonio stopped, taking a deep whiff of the sultry air.

"What's wrong?" Tyler said. "Are you okay?"

"I'm fine. Just keep going."

Within a few more steps Antonio stopped short again, breathing deeply.

"What are you doing?" Kathy asked.

He stared at her and for a split second he looked crazed—his eyes chilled her to the bone.

"What's wrong with you?" she asked.

He paused, shook his head, looking somewhat more normal.

"The heat's getting to me, that's all."

Up ahead a small suspension bridge spanned a stagnant moat. Beyond, the castle loomed so colossal in size it was impossible to view its entire extent.

Tyler felt in his pocket as they approached the bridge. "Get your flutes ready," he said. "We're going to need them."

"That's for sure," Leonard said. "I just hope the flutes are strong enough to keep them at bay."

"Don't worry, just use what we've been taught," Tyler said.

Step by step they began to walk across the wooden bridge. The sheer size of Jedermann's domain intimidated them, making them feel like tiny ants. Tyler took a deep breath, leading them over the murky waters. They peered down into the moat; the steam rising from the water seemed to warn them that they were entering dangerous territory. They came to the opposite end of the bridge, without signs of Jedermann or Seirens.

"Why haven't they tried to stop us?" Kathy asked. They looked at each other and shrugged. "This can't be good," she said.

By the time they reached solid ground outside the castle walls Antonio was breathing deeply again.

Tyler and Leonard exchanged worried glances. Antonio was sweating more profusely than the rest of them. Some of his hair spikes fell forward, plastered to the beads of sweat on his forehead; his eyes had the look of a wild animal.

154

Cautiously, they ventured from shadow to shadow like guerilla fighters. "Shhh!" Tyler said, "Listen."

They all heard it—the irregular beating of drums. With each step through the growing gloom the noise grew louder. Kathy covered her ears at the sounds of violins playing horribly off-key.

"Follow those beats," Antonio ordered in an unusually raspy voice, pointing toward a long curved wall.

Kathy shot a questioning look at Tyler.

Antonio walked faster and faster toward the ruckus, as though under a spell. The others felt repulsed by the noise, fearful of what may loom beyond.

"Wait, Antonio!" Tyler shouted, running to catch up with him. Leonard kept his pace slower to stay with Kathy. Antonio ran up a massive stone staircase leading up high behind the front wall, following the chaotic sounds, not even looking back at the others.

"Wait for us!" Tyler called, but Antonio continued up the stairs out of sight. He tossed the small flute far behind him, almost hitting Kathy. She picked it up, looking puzzled.

"WHAT ARE YOU THINKING, MAN?!" Tyler yelled. "We're gonna' need that! Wait up!"

Antonio bounded to the top and gasped at the scene below. Young people of all ages danced and beat on drums, running wildly in the light of torches. On a far balcony beyond the courtyard, Antonio saw Jedermann himself, dramatic in his black cape. He waved a black wand toward him causing Antonio's vision to distort, leaving him disoriented. Some of the victims below suddenly looked like his friends back home—the ones who wanted him kicked out of their band. They waved to him, inviting him to come down. He was filled with a desire to join them.

When Tyler reached the top, he stopped, stunned. The

flaming torches ignited strange feelings within him. He approached Antonio, who coldly ignored him.

Antonio stared into the crowds, thinking it looked like a fun party, with uninhibited freedom.

"Tony, didn't you hear me?" Tyler asked. "They're out of their minds down there. Look at how they're fighting."

Jedermann spotted Tyler and waved his black baton over them both. A chill spread silently, invisibly across their bodies. The scene below seemed to change for Tyler, too. He thought, *Looks like they're not having such a bad time after all.*

Kathy and Leonard arrived at the top of the stairs, panting. Their eyes opened wide at the sight of the chaos below. "Oh, God!" Leonard exclaimed.

"I can't bear to watch," Kathy said, turning away, covering her ears.

"But look at Tyler and Antonio. They're mesmerized. What's happening to them?"

"All our visitors have arrived! Welcome!" Jedermann shouted to the throng below, pointing the baton at the Messengers. The masses below beckoned them with out-stretched arms.

"Hey, you up there!" yelled one of the boys. "Come on down! We follow no rules here. We get to do anything we want!"

"Yes! Come join the other children—the ones who know how to enjoy themselves!" Jedermann jabbed the baton at the new arrivals, waving it in circles through the air toward them, causing strange thoughts to whirl through their minds like funnel clouds.

I'm powerless to fight this, Tyler thought. *Maybe I can be cool like Antonio for once in my life.* His own mission to save his sister and the Gold Baton vanished from his mind. And the sacred instruments? Who cared? His purpose in Orphea became smothered by the folds of Jedermann's flowing cloak.

He thought about his father's judgmental eyes upon him. *Why doesn't dad ever let me make my own choices? People have complete freedom here.*

Antonio looked at Tyler in a friendlier way. "Hey, maybe this is our chance for the ultimate adventure."

Maybe Antonio's right, Tyler thought. *Maybe this is my chance to fit in completely.* "You're right, Antonio," he said. "I can't keep living in the past. We've always done fun stuff together our whole lives. Why not this?"

"Now you're sounding more like the kind of friend I've always wanted," Antonio answered.

"Tyler!" Leonard yelled, but he didn't listen.

The young people below writhed and twisted into grotesque shapes. Kathy felt sick to her stomach. The conservatory students of Orphea in the mob looked very much like her friends, but their eyes shone bewitched and glassy, their behavior out of control. Frightening hissing Seirens hid in the shadows with monsters of all shapes and sizes. She pulled Leonard closer to her and begged Tyler, "Can't you see what's happening down there? Stop looking. Please!"

But then Kathy lost her focus. Her curiosity tempted her to glance for a moment too long. Leonard squeezed her hand to help her concentrate and it worked for a few moments. She gazed down at the sacred instruments on the heap of wood and the sounds of music overtook her mind. She had a vivid flash of Liszt's hands on the piano and the overpowering inspiration she'd felt from his playing.

Jedermann sensed Kathy's internal strength. "Want to see what I call stylish? Watch this!" He whipped the baton savagely at her, then turned it on a group of teen girls standing below her, transforming their dirty rags into sleek, glittery garments.

Kathy felt pleasantly shocked that they suddenly resembled her with fashionable clothing and dazzling jewelry. "Look, Leonard! That girl's even got boots like mine!" Kathy continued gazing at the girls, entranced at the parade of fashion, more dazzling than she'd ever seen, while Jedermann smiled. Peculiar thoughts threatened to possess her. *Don't people live forever here? Maybe this isn't such a bad place after all.*

Several boys stared at Leonard. "Hey, scientist!" they jeered. "In case you're counting on magic to save you, there's no such thing as magic—white magic, that is. And science won't save you either. Won't you join us and have some fun? It's terrible to die alone in the end."

Jedermann hurled more energy from the baton toward Leonard, but he didn't waver for a split second. Instead he focused on bringing his friends back to themselves.

A young girl circled the endangered instruments on the woodpile. Another boy joined her. "No more being slaves to practice, practice, practice," the boy said, "once those instruments are burned."

"That's for sure," the girl agreed. "We make our own decisions here." She joined others wandering aimlessly, doing nothing. Amathes began to walk through the crowd, scowling and hissing, clawing at the young zombies. Other Seirens came out and circled the throngs, stirring up trouble between them, enticing them to fight.

Tyler's rebellious train of thought, influenced by Jedermann, continued. *Dad can never find anything good to say about me. And, besides, he never treated Mom right, either—or Christina.* The instant his sister's name rang in his mind, he saw a flicker of light dance across his French horn below. He recalled with a sudden flash the joy he'd felt playing his horn for the first time, with Dr. Fuddle watching him. In his mind he heard the music of his horn and felt the empowerment playing it had given him—the truest sense of freedom he'd ever felt. His gaze remained fixed on his horn and he focused his mind on the memory of its music.

Then something unexpected happened. A thought flashed

through Tyler's mind—the thought of the rose petals and his sister's dance with the gnomes. The power of that joyful memory sent vibrations across the courtyard. Several young people below felt it, and their own memories were rekindled. They looked at one another, surprised. Several lifted their instruments into the air and began to play music—a sweet music resonating of hope. A group of small children began to sing harmoniously as they gazed upon Tyler and the others standing on the high ledge. The evil spell was breaking.

But Jedermann noticed and cracked the black baton into the air, instantly disrupting the music of the children, dashing their hopes to pieces. "I command you to stop!" The eyes of his victims grew dark once more and their music turned to chaos—with shrieks and wails of clashing dissonance. Seirens and the other dismal creatures joined in on the noise, like cats screeching at a full moon. The rhythmless beats of the drums joined in the cacophony. Jedermann howled eerily, looking at the small figures standing on the wall. "Come join us! Are you willing?" His voice was sickeningly sweet. A sense of unrest grew with his every move.

Tyler stayed unmoving by Antonio's side.

Leonard put his arms around Kathy and whispered, "Kathy, please. Come with me. Don't be tricked again. There's nothing good down there. You have a choice in this."

She turned around and he grabbed her hands. The combination of his physical touch and the compassion in his voice was like music to her. She looked into his eyes and saw that same captivating look as when he'd played his cello successfully for Bach the first time. She knew she could never forget his expression making that music. Her head snapped back up. Her eyes were clear and sparkling again.

"Don't worry. I won't be tricked again," she said, focusing on her viola down below, her resolve so great Leonard knew he'd never have to worry about her again.

Jedermann's eyes narrowed to slits. He sent thoughts to Amathes and Aplestos. *We're losing the little hero for now— we've lost control over him and he's thinking of his sister and music. Focus on the pretty boy instead. He's OURS.* Aplestos flew into the crowd and picked out two prized specimens—a tall twelve-year-old boy and a stunning fourteen-year-old girl. She lifted them up and flew them close to where Antonio stood, suspending them in mid-air. Jedermann released more energy from the baton blurring Antonio's thoughts even more, strengthening the gruesome delusion.

"You'll be like a god here," the fourteen-year-old girl called to him. "Come with us."

"You'll love it here," the boy said, as he swayed in the air in Aplestos' grasp.

Tyler ran between Antonio and the two children pulling for his soul. "Resist, Antonio, you've got to resist! It's all an illusion—a mind trick. Think about Dr. Fuddle and all the great music he taught us to play. There's nothing good about this place. They're appealing to our darker side."

Aplestos moved in closer dangling the girl with the long dark hair. She reached for Antonio's hand, her eyes black like Jedermann's but hauntingly beautiful. Antonio became enchanted and moved closer to her and thought *if this is my darker side, I want more of it...*

Tyler grabbed his sweaty shoulder.

"GET OFF ME!" Antonio growled, never taking his face away from the girl's. He struck Tyler's chest with his elbow, sending him reeling backwards. "You're not spoiling my fun this time, Tyler! You've never been cool. You've embarrassed me since the first grade." The pain from Antonio's cruel words stung far worse than the pain from his fall. Tyler picked himself up, his face red with anger.

"Antonio! We're the ones who care about you," Kathy

160

urged in vain. He walked away from his friends, closer to the edge of the stone wall, toward the alluring images of the hovering girl and boy. The deafening tempo of the drumbeats increased, urging him forward. He lifted his foot onto the ledge. A disturbing smile crept over his face. His piercing dark eyes turned a cloudy gray in the light of the burning torches.

Antonio Romero

He turned around, drew a deep breath and smiled at Tyler—a smile so frightening, Tyler shuddered.

161

"We can't win this, Tyler," he said, spellbound past the point of no return. "I'm going willingly. It's the thrill of a lifetime. No need to be forced."

While Antonio gazed below the strange words from the sign at the entrance to Dis haunted Tyler's mind. *And if you're not willing...* Over and over he heard the words as if it had become a threatening chant rising from the bedlam below. He watched Jedermann's Seirens beckon to them, with hunger in their eyes. Aplestos hovered with the boy and girl, calling to Antonio.

Tyler's will was very strong by this point. His mission was fixed and unmovable in his mind. He spoke slowly, with authority. "We were chosen to save Orphea, Antonio. Turn away now. Please. Come with us."

Antonio opened his arms wide to reach for Tyler, as if to hug him. Tyler eagerly went to him, relieved. But the moment Antonio's hands touched him, he felt repulsed by their icy coldness and quickly jerked away.

"They're going to have us anyway," Antonio said, in a voice no longer his own. "We can't win. Let's go willingly."

Tyler was frantic, "No, Antonio! Don't look at them! You can resist, like we did. We've got to stay on track!"

Kathy took one last look at Antonio, horrified. "Forget about trying to convince him, Tyler. He's dangerous! He's no longer one of us."

"That's right, Tyler. It's too late," Antonio whispered in Tyler's ear. And in the blink of an eye, Antonio turned and threw himself head first over the ledge, into the welcoming arms of Jedermann's throngs below.

Chapter Twenty

Dazed, Tyler backed away from the ledge. He wiped tears from his eyes but knew he had no time to grieve over the loss of his best friend. "Come on," he said to Leonard and Kathy. "We've got to find Christina."

They bounded down the steps and searched frantically for a way into the castle. Tyler spotted an opening several hundred yards from where they stood. "This way," he said, leading them past several sections of the castle toward a small entrance. The drumbeats faded in the distance.

Kathy held back a scream as they rounded the corner. A fierce looking saber-toothed Seiren was sitting outside the entrance, blocking the opening.

Tyler reached for his flute. "Wait." Leonard instantly caught on and got his musical pipe ready, too. "Let's hope this works."

"It will," Tyler said.

They inched closer toward the Seiren. It was slumped to the side, eyes closed, with a club held loosely in one hand.

"What's it doing?" Kathy asked.

"I guess it's supposed to be guarding the entrance," Leonard said.

"Fortunately, for us, it's not doing a very good job," Tyler watched the Seiren closely. "He looks asleep to me."

A faint smile escaped from Kathy's lips as she brought her flute out of her pocket.

Tyler led them even closer then stopped, raising the flute. "Let's use the Bach *Minuet*," he said. "That worked with the captive Seirens."

Kathy and Leonard held their instruments tight, ready to play, while Tyler raised the flute to his mouth. "I'll play the opening voice," he said, "and Leonard, you join me in the bass voice and Kathy the top voice. Ready?"

Tyler performed the opening notes. Even though Leonard missed his entrance, he made it in time for the second half of his phrase. The Seiren shifted slightly. By the time Kathy's top voice came in the Seiren woke up and looked around. Each tone Tyler played sounded sweet. His mind flashed back to Dr. Fuddle playing his mother's special tune on his piano in the beautiful light-filled room of the mansion—how he and his friends were filled with a sense of wellbeing in meeting their mentor. He focused on that vision in his mind, proceeding through the piece with Kathy and Leonard. And as they played, they crept closer, moving in on the Seiren. By the time they were half way through the piece the Seiren dropped its club, its frightening appearance gone. The saber teeth changed to normal sized feline teeth, and by the end of the minuet it looked as gentle as a kitten.

"Good work!" Tyler said. "Okay, make a run for it!" They raced through the doorway, into the dark, dank smelling castle. Torches lit up a cavernous passageway. Tyler took the lead, while Leonard and Kathy followed.

"That wasn't so bad," Kathy said.

"We were better than I thought we'd be." Leonard agreed.

Tyler smiled. "Looks like we aced our first Seiren test."

"And we hit those eighth notes precisely," Kathy said, looking back at the subdued Seiren. "And that thing's bad smell even went away. Amazing."

Directly ahead stood a small gate made of iron, leading farther underground.

"We've got to keep our sense of direction," Tyler said. "We have to head toward the courtyard area. I think we can sense our way."

They expected relief from the sweltering heat when they stepped farther into the tunnel, but didn't find it. The air felt hotter than ever. Tyler used his instincts to lead the way through the main passageway, well into the interior of the castle before stopping in a large open area. More torches hung from the walls casting haunting shadows in all directions around them. Several tunnels led away into the darkness.

"Which way?" Kathy asked.

"Come on, this way," Tyler urged, but then stopped his friends. "Let me check it out, first. Stay here." A deep pit lay ahead. "Not this way," he said, checking two other tunnels for safe passage. Tyler made sure the coast was clear before he motioned for his friends to proceed down the widest tunnel that showed the most signs of traffic.

They hid behind a wall when they heard footsteps farther down the corridor. The trio waited until the sound of the steps faded into silence before they cautiously moved ahead.

At the end of another tunnel they spotted two more guards. They held their breath and huddled silently until the Seirens roamed away completely out of sight. "Whew," Kathy said, relieved, not knowing if they could handle two at once. "How are we ever going to find Christina?" she whispered. "This is a hopeless maze!"

"We've just got to keep looking until we find signs of her," Tyler said.

From around the corner they heard a scraping noise. It lasted only a second, forcing them to freeze in their tracks.

"Don't move," Tyler urged.

They stood breathless until they heard the sound again—this time it moved closer.

Kathy reached for Leonard's hand.

There was silence again, then more shuffling noises before the sounds stopped. Then footsteps.

As the steps grew closer, Kathy raised her flute, dropping Leonard's hand. Each passing second seemed agonizing. Her confidence from their first Seiren victory faded quickly. Leonard's fingers tightened around his flute as the steps approached. Tyler stood ready for action.

Then, slowly, the tip of an instrument appeared with a small arm attached to it.

Their blood ran cold as they waited.

Suddenly, the friendly face of the lead-dancing gnome appeared.

"Shhh!" he whispered. "Be very quiet, this place is riddled with guards."

They were stunned.

"Erkenbald! What are you doing here?" Tyler said. He was so shocked he hardly knew what to say.

Kathy was so happy she wanted to kiss the little gnome.

"Don't you remember?" he said.

"Remember?" Leonard asked.

"Yes—about the task force."

"You're the task force?" Tyler said.

"Not just me—all of my gnome brothers are here, ready to rescue the sacred instruments before they burn them." He looked at Tyler. "I'm afraid we haven't been able to find your sister yet." Kathy reached for Tyler's hand. "But don't worry, we will."

Tyler nodded, though it was obvious to the others he was worried.

"Come with me," Erkenbald said, looking down a nearby tunnel. "Let's talk."

He led them through a tight passage and into a musty chamber.

Tyler looked back to make sure they hadn't been followed. "But don't you know…" His voice broke, reliving the nightmarish sight of Dr. Fuddle turning to dust. "Don't you know what happened on the bridge?"

"We know everything." Erkenbald struggled to overcome his grief.

"You do?" they all said at once.

"Yes. And even though the attacks have grown worse, it hasn't stopped the army from advancing. They're approaching even now."

"Really?" Kathy and Leonard said at the same time, excited by the news.

"Yes."

"But can we succeed without Dr. Fuddle?" Tyler asked, not ashamed of his tears.

The gnome nodded his disproportionately large head. "We must do what we can."

"You're right," Tyler answered.

"Unfortunately, Juliet and Elizabeth have fallen under the spell and will need our help, too," Erkenbald sighed.

"Our poor friends," Kathy said. "We've got to free them too."

"But there's good news," Erkenbald said. "There's something you don't know about dancing gnomes and Seirens." The gnome managed a smile, hoping to partially ease their pain.

"What's that?" Tyler asked.

167

"They don't mix! We gnomes can't stand cats of any kind. They're about the only animal we can't abide. And if there's one thing a Seiren can't stand, it's the sight of a gnome. We drive them crazy like flies on a cow's nose! They even hate the smell of us. And being spies, we know every inch of this castle. That's why we were given the job of getting your instruments back."

Hope never burned brighter in Tyler's face.

Erkenbald led them out of the chamber. "Move quickly. We don't have much time." He craned his neck to look into the next passageway and motioned for everyone to follow. "Keep those flutes ready. We're going for Christina first."

"Leonard?" Tyler whispered. "Do you think we can trust him? Maybe he's a shape-shifting Seiren."

Leonard took a second to respond and put his hand on Tyler's shoulder.

"Tyler, my friend, sometimes you just have to trust."

They bumped fists and smiled. Never did Tyler think he'd hear those words from Leonard.

The three stole their way down the tunnel, walking closely behind the gnome. Tyler and Leonard walked on either side of Kathy, flutes ready. A guard could be seen in the distance. They raised their flutes.

"Back," said the gnome, motioning everyone against a wall.

Two more Seiren guards walked toward the first one and all three went around the corner.

"Where are they going?" Tyler asked.

"They're securing all passageways surrounding the courtyard."

"How many guards are there?" Leonard asked.

"Too many. I knocked out two with tritones, but now that you're here we can take on more at one time."

Kathy moved closer to Leonard.

"Just walk slowly behind me and don't make a sound," urged the gnome, edging closer to the end of the tunnel. They huddled near the doorway of a five-sided room, guarded by saber-toothed Seirens. They remained quietly in the shadows, before the gnome motioned everyone to backtrack a few steps.

"How are we ever going to get past so many guards?" Kathy moaned.

"Well we can't just run by them," Leonard said. "We've got to use our music."

Before Tyler could say another word, music echoed in the tunnel. The guards stiffened and listened, then recoiled, running away.

"Only one thing makes them run," Tyler said hopefully. "Music!"

"Might be our troops," Erkenbald whispered.

They tiptoed to the vacated spot and came to an empty cell, its gate open. They stopped. No more music. Tyler saw it first. They walked into the cell and he picked it up, then dropped it. It was a torn swatch of material—a floral print from Christina's dress. He wiped a tear and looked questioningly at the others.

"That must mean she's escaped!" Kathy exclaimed.

"Or...worse," Leonard muttered.

Erkenbald looked solemn and concerned.

None of them dared to imagine the worst.

Chapter Twenty-One

Tyler looked as if he would explode—with grief, rage, fear, hatred. He attempted to dash through the cell door, but Leonard held him back. Tyler struggled, "Let me go! I've got to find Christina!"

"No, Ty, no! You won't do us any good running right into the claws of powerful Seirens alone. Get a hold of yourself." Leonard held him firmly while Kathy hugged his shoulder. He slumped in misery.

"You're right. Give me a second." He walked around the cell, breathing deeply, his back to the others. He picked up the floral material and put it into his pocket.

Then suddenly, from a distant tunnel, they heard a faint "Hello! My name is Dolly!"

"It's Christina!" Kathy said in a hushed whisper. Tyler started to take off again.

"Wait!" Leonard said, grabbing his arm. "A Seiren might have pulled that string on the doll." Tyler didn't want to believe that, but knew it could be true.

"Leonard's right, Tyler," Erkenbald said. "We can't take anything for granted."

The group inched their way down the tunnel, stopping

only when they saw Christina being dragged away in the distance. Both her arms were being held by Seirens as they pulled her along the passageway.

"Let her go!" Tyler yelled, unable to control himself.

With the sound of his voice, the Seirens turned. The two holding her whisked her out of sight, while several other Seirens made an about face, racing toward Tyler and his friends.

"Follow me," Erkenbald instructed. "And keep your flutes ready."

They raced their way behind Erkenbald, only to come upon three more Seirens.

"Hang on!" Erkenbald shouted. And before they knew it, he'd suspended all of them from the ceiling twenty feet above.

"How did you do that?" Tyler groaned, the rocks digging into his back.

Kathy held onto her glasses.

"Gnome magic," Erkenbald said. "Just be as still as possible."

The pack of Seirens raced below, looking for them in all directions. Two stopped. Tyler held his breath praying they wouldn't look up. Finally the two scurried off and out of sight.

"This won't be comfortable," Erkenbald said. "But we'll have to scoot along the ceiling upside down on our hands and knees. The Seirens aren't smart enough to look up."

Blood rushed to their heads as they made their way to a wide empty tunnel. They heard music—this time a soft violin melody, a Bach gavotte.

With the sound of the music, several Seiren guards bellowed in the distance. Their excited shrieks faded as they disappeared, until the only sound left was that of the violin.

"This is our chance." Erkenbald yelled. "Come on! I know where the music is coming from."

They dropped from the ceiling and rushed down the hallway after the gnome, flutes ready for action. The sound of their footsteps alerted two more Seirens, who chased after them.

Tyler and Leonard ran on either side of Erkenbald, playing minor seconds then resolving them to thirds as fast as they could blow. Kathy followed right behind resolving scales fast and furiously, the Seirens at her heels.

They howled at the sounds, and swiped with their wings, trying to knock the flutes out of their hands. One taller Seiren succeeded in grabbing Kathy's ankle, making her trip. The flute flew out of her hand and just before a Seiren could grab it, Tyler and Leonard resolved scales in unison. It withdrew its hand just as Tyler grabbed the flute. Leonard freed Kathy from its grip.

"Hurry!" yelled the gnome, leading them around another corner.

"Come on, run!" Tyler shouted. They followed the gnome down a narrow passage, finally outrunning the Seirens, their music having weakened them. The heat was intense as they rushed along, sweating and panting.

"In here!" Erkenbald yelled, leading them through a tight opening, into a hidden chamber where a wonderful sight greeted them.

There stood Juliet and Elizabeth with Christina and Dolly safe in their arms.

"Christina, Christina!" Tyler yelled, trying to keep his voice down. Her dress was tattered and torn, but otherwise she looked unharmed. Juliet and Elizabeth kissed her on the head, before releasing her to Tyler. "You all right? You still have Dolly! You still have your writing pad?"

Christina smiled, revealing the pad from an inner pocket, then tucking it away.

Leonard and Kathy joined Tyler, hugging Christina.

Tyler held his sister tight. Leonard stood at the opening, watching the flicker of every torch for any movement in the shadows.

"How did you do it?" Tyler asked Juliet. "I can't thank you enough! Erkenbald said you were under Jedermann's spell."

"No," Elizabeth said. "Are you kidding? We're stronger than that!"

"Well, we were despondent at first, beginning to give up hope—it was taking you so long to get here," Juliet said.

"But when we saw them bring in Christina, we knew you wouldn't be far behind," Elizabeth added.

"So we pretended to be in their stupid trance so they wouldn't lock us up!"

"Smart thinking!" Leonard exclaimed.

"They got me out of the cell with their violin music," Christina wrote.

Kathy hugged both of the girls and by that time everyone was hopeful again.

"Let's plan quickly," Tyler said. "I've got an idea."

"Explain," Leonard requested.

"With all due respect, Erkenbald, to you and your friends," Tyler said, "since we were the ones responsible for losing the sacred instruments, I believe it's our rightful duty to get them back. And fast." Erkenbald smiled and nodded. "We'll hide in an archway leading to the courtyard," Tyler said to his friends. "And you," he continued, talking to the gnome, "it's time to gather the other gnomes and hide in strategic positions, ready to distract the Seirens guarding the instruments."

"And then?" Leonard asked.

"Just give us a signal of three short tones and a long tone of Beethoven's *Fifth* and I'll make a run for my horn with Juliet and Elizabeth behind me playing their violins for reinforcement," Tyler said. "Then everyone make a dash for your instruments. Once you have them in hand, break into Beethoven's *Grosse Fugue* while I grab Antonio's drum. That should hold back the Seirens and buy us some time until the musical army gets here."

"But do you really think this will work?" Kathy asked. "There are so many of them."

"It has to, Kathy," Tyler said. "It's our only chance." She nodded.

Erkenbald shook his hand, inspired by their courage.

Kathy appeared hesitant at first. "Okay. I'm willing to take the risk for Dr. Fuddle's sake."

Tyler beamed at her. "We *will* save Orphea!" His confidence was so strong it became contagious. *If it's the last thing we ever do he thought.*

"You're saving all that's good and beautiful," Juliet said. Christina nodded her head with full assurance.

"This is in honor of Dr. Fuddle," Leonard added. He looked at the gnome. "You think this is a good strategy?"

"Better than what we had planned to do."

"What was that?"

"Just dance, dance, dance in circles and hope for the best!"

Tyler smiled at the others, not knowing if he was joking.

The gnome continued. "I think we have an excellent chance once you have the sacred instruments. That fugue may even transform a number of the Seirens. By then our support should be here."

"We have to keep trusting and be ready to play this by ear," Tyler said, "just in case anything unexpected happens."

"You are wise and courageous beyond your years," Erkenbald said. "Just listen for our musical signal. Does everyone understand what to do?" They nodded.

"If the forces of Orpheus are with us, the orchestral army will already have gathered on the other side of the gates."

"Tyler, you think we can get Antonio back?" Leonard asked.

"We can only hope he isn't too far gone," Tyler said solemnly.

In silence, they followed the gnome out of the chamber. "I marked the main tunnel leading to the courtyard with a small star in case you need to find it without me," he said.

They walked steadily through the dank passageway, checking for Seirens hiding in the shadows at every step. Halfway down, they heard the unbalanced drumbeats from the courtyard. Christina put her hands over her ears.

"We're almost there," the gnome said, pointing to a hanging torch ahead. "When we get to that torch, stop and we'll size up the ground conditions."

As they neared the torch, they heard chanting. Over and over the ominous words rang in their ears:

"Und bist du nicht willig, so brauch ich gewalt!"

"They're chanting what was on the sign," Kathy said, "and if you're not willing, I'll use force!" Their dissonant sounds made her feel sick.

When the little group arrived at the torch, they stopped as Erkenbald had instructed. Every one glanced back and seeing that they had not been followed, looked out into the courtyard. Christina's eyes danced with hope under the torch.

But the scene before them had deteriorated into an even more ghastly sight than before. Around the woodpile, the throngs had been driven into a wild frenzy. Some of the smaller children were frightened out of their minds and hiding, spell or no spell. Tyler wished he could block the view from the girls but knew he couldn't. It was the first time he had ever seen rage in the eyes of his sister.

While they crouched hidden in the tunnel, Jedermann stood in the courtyard, towering over everyone as though he were a mighty king. His black cloak flowed behind him like snakes. An obsidian crown stood on top of his head. His gnarled hand grasped the blackened baton and like a master puppeteer, he conducted every move of his subjects. With a slight turn of his wrist he forced violent movements. Antonio's body twisted with the others. He hardly looked human.

Kathy gasped, seeing him. "Oh, no!" Tyler's hand covered her mouth, so she wouldn't give away their position. But a Seiren in a neighboring corridor had already perked up his ears. Kathy stared in horror at the danger ahead, reaching once more for Leonard's hand, but not finding it.

From his position on high, Jedermann glared at Amathes and Aplestos. "Have you captured the so-called Messengers yet? I must know their whereabouts before we can proceed!"

"No, Master," Amathes admitted, cowering in fear.

"*WHAT?*" Jedermann shouted into his face. "Shall I have you burned, too?"

"But Master! We've looked everywhere for them and they're nowhere to be found."

"Impossible, you fool! I must have them in chains before we begin the burning ceremony!"

"We know, Master, but…"

"Stop making excuses!" Jedermann waved the baton more madly than ever. He glared into the anxious faces of his top commanders. "Your incompetence will not disrupt my crowning moment!"

Jedermann paused, distracted, looking down at his subjects, relishing how they went into fits in the toxic surroundings, watching many of them trample their instruments under their feet. Then he came back to the present moment. "Find them now! Do you hear me? NOW!"

The longer Tyler and his friends watched the sick spectacle, the hotter grew their anger. Tyler flushed with rage, seeing Antonio manipulated like a rag doll by the sheer force of Jedermann's dark power.

"We haven't a moment to lose," Erkenbald said. "Don't worry. Stay here and wait for the signal." Off he rushed to gather the other gnomes, knowing exactly how to find them to position them for the assault.

Tyler and the others waited, looking at their instruments in the woodpile not too far away and watched for the gnomes. Unseen by them, one Seiren scurried closer. Kathy fixed her eyes on her viola, not daring to look at the fashionable girls she'd been attracted to earlier. Aplestos crept into position near her. Leonard looked at his cello, longing to play it. Yet another Seiren positioned himself nearby.

Kathy, seeing the gnomes there to help, turned to say, "I think this is going to work, don't you?" But Aplestos' paw covered Kathy's mouth before she could speak, while another Seiren grabbed her by her hair and seized her flute. Behind her, Leonard, Elizabeth and Juliet were in the clutches of other Seirens, their mouths gagged with dirty cloths, their instruments also ripped from their hands.

Tyler and Christina remained unaware of the danger behind them.

"The greatest musicians of Orphea will soon come here to help us," Tyler said to Christina, whose face suddenly warned of impending doom. "And everything will be all right."

"Don't think that's going to happen any time soon," whispered a raspy voice in his ear. He turned around to look up at Amathes' Bengal tiger grin. He felt he'd pass out. "I'll take that now, if you please," Amathes said, snatching Tyler's flute with no effort, adding it to his collection from the others. He then motioned for more guards, who grabbed Christina and dragged her into the opening for Jedermann to see.

Aplestos and Amathes stepped forward with Tyler and

Kathy in their clutches. Another Seiren gripped Leonard. "They've all been captured, Master!" Aplestos said, while Amathes tossed the flutes onto the woodpile.

Jedermann laughed raucously. "Lift them up where everyone can see my trophies!" He cheered as his two top commanders and the Saber-toothed Seirens raised them high up into the air—the struggling Messengers of Music—Orphea's last hope.

Captured.

Chapter Twenty-Two

"This is far from over." Tyler's whisper felt more like an announcement than mere words of encouragement. The Seirens had imprisoned them deep within the dungeon. He managed to free his hands to untie the gag, leaving swollen red streaks on his face. He threw the rag into a corner, ready to untie Leonard, when the guard paced past their cell again. Its claws retracted with all four paws padding on the dirt floor. Kathy wrinkled her nose at his strong odor as he prowled by. Tyler feigned sleep with his head down, away from the guard's eyes. The moment the Seiren's back was turned he freed Leonard.

Tyler and Leonard quickly unloosed the girls. Elizabeth mumbled, urgently trying to say something while Tyler took off her gag.

"What, Elizabeth?" he whispered.

"Christina's still got a..." She glanced cautiously at the guard, who turned and strode back their way on his rounds.

Elizabeth pointed to Christina, who revealed the spare

flute she'd kept hidden in Dolly's pinafore. The top of it stuck out. When the guard came closer, they assumed their tied up positions, heads down. Once his back was turned, marching in the other direction, they whispered.

"So who's going to be the one to use it?" Kathy asked.

Christina handed the flute to Tyler, deciding the issue at once. His glow of confidence calmed everyone's nerves. Tyler never felt less afraid in his life, even with setback after setback. He lifted the flute to his lips. He knew exactly what to do. Something told him not to begin with the crashing first notes that opened the *Grosse Fugue*. Instead he played the soft notes that came afterward. The Seiren turned around, its cat eyes scanning the area.

"Keep playing," Leonard said. They all gathered at the cell bars. This time Tyler blew the loud opening of the fugue, the notes piercing the air like daggers. The Seiren growled and bounded back to their cell. They took a good look at the Saber-tooth's face. It looked almost human, not nearly as revolting as some of the others.

Then Tyler blasted the fugue like a shotgun. The first A-flat hit the Seiren like a grenade. He looked crazed and grunted again, this time in pain. Tyler relentlessly blasted the top voice of the fugue. The Seiren couldn't make up his mind what to do.

"Hey!" Kathy yelled. "Let's sing the other parts!"

"Great idea!" Leonard said.

While Tyler continued to blast his part, the others sang and clapped and stomped the rhythms of the other three parts. The Seiren's head began to weave back and forth, and it stretched its long neck, like it was trying to join in the song. Small sounds gurgled from its mouth. Its eyes changed. It was clear to everyone the music was transforming the Seiren right before their eyes. It lifted its wings, as though to take off into flight, dropping the key from its paw a few feet away outside the cell. Christina fell to the floor and reached for it through the bars.

"Stretch, Christina, stretch!" Tyler urged.

She stretched her small arm as far as it would go, but it wouldn't quite reach. Tyler blasted four more notes and the Seiren's back paw gave one powerful spasm, pushing the key just within Christina's reach, before running off down the tunnel.

Christina grabbed the key and held it up as though she'd won the gold ring.

"It's a miracle!" Leonard shouted. He composed himself, looking half embarrassed by his sudden outburst. "Well, it certainly wasn't luck, that's for sure."

The others cheered.

Tyler turned the key and opened the door of the cell.

"Great job!" Kathy exclaimed.

"But we'd better hurry. Come on!" Tyler shouted. He ran through the tunnel as fast as his legs would carry him, the others right behind him. They turned corner after corner, raced up a flight of winding steps, around another corner, and then toward the star-marked tunnel that led to the courtyard frenzy.

** ** ** ** **

"Finally!" Jedermann shouted. He watched the Seirens return without the Messengers of Music. "Have you imprisoned them?"

"Yes, Master. They're securely locked in the dungeon," Aplestos answered. "But wouldn't you rather have them in chains out here to witness the destruction of their prizes?"

"No! They've caused me more than enough trouble. Are you sure they're unable to escape?"

"Of course, Master. All locked up. We wouldn't fail you again. We left a guard just in case," Amathes added.

"Only ONE? Make it two, no three, no—one for each one of them! And I'm warning you, never make me wait again!" He watched several more Seiren guards being dispatched into a tunnel. "Excellent. We may now begin our final preparations."

Amathes and Aplestos stood before the enormous heap of wood. Jedermann raised the blackened scepter of harmony, guiding his mob of victims around to watch from all sides. Seirens of all shapes and sizes emerged from the shadows, some flying, some growling low growls and leaping on all fours. They cheered, shrieking their chants high into the air while the drummers pounded savagely. Many of the children of Orphea seemed too afraid to look at the sacred instruments, although some dared to peek.

Jedermann let out a mighty roar of delight: "To the Forces of Cacophony, I dedicate these instruments to the successful downfall of Dr. Benjamin Erastus Fuddle!"

A guard flew out of the surrounding darkness with a torch in its paw.

"Come, beautiful boy," Jedermann commanded to Antonio. "I anoint you to set the fire!" Antonio, no longer resembling his former self at all, stepped up. He robotically obeyed, but fixed his eyes on the instruments across the way. Jedermann watched him closely, ready with the baton in hand to strike if necessary, in case the sight of his drum awakened him.

Aplestos and Amathes lifted him up on their shoulders carrying him toward the awaiting woodpile, with the girl and boy who'd beckoned him earlier not far behind. They set him down by the woodpile. He accepted the large torch. The Seirens cheered, spinning around him wildly. The flames danced in his eyes, casting dark shadows on his face, distorting his fine features into something vile. Sweat dripped from his body. His spikes had completely vanished, his hair wet and plastered against his head.

"Light the fire! Spread the flames!" Jedermann commanded.

Amathes leaped for joy and Aplestos wailed and waved her wings into the air. At the exact moment Antonio saw the cello and viola his expression changed ever so slightly. Then he looked at the horn and his own drum awaiting the fire. For a moment he felt passion sweep through him—like the time when his drum had first responded to his beating heart.

Jedermann watched him closely, eyes narrowing. "Pound our drums! The time has come!" he commanded.

Antonio had a vision of Dolly staring at him and a flash of Christina pulling Dolly's string, joining their pact for victory.

Hundreds of hypnotized children gathered behind the Seirens. They looked at Antonio with fear in their eyes.

His torch neared the wood and a thought streaked into his mind as he looked at Jedermann: *Your power cannot make me do this.*

Jedermann's Seiren guards stood close to Antonio. The cheers of Amathes and Aplestos egged him on. Antonio was now one of the leaders. Jedermann pointed at him with the baton. Antonio lowered the torch to the wood. A huge roar of approval erupted from the Seirens. The children of Orphea stood silent. Flames shot onto the piece of wood that burned brightly, igniting piece after piece.

"LET THE DESTRUCTION BEGIN!" Jedermann cheered, pointing to the instruments with the black baton. Antonio's eyes darted from Aplestos and Amathes to his drum. It felt as though he could hear its rich rhythmic tones resounding from the crackle of wood that was slowly but steadily catching on fire, ready to devour the instruments.

Jedermann's drummers pounded louder than ever. The ground shook with the stomping Seirens. Thunderous cheers erupted at the sight of the fire moving closer and closer to the instruments. "To the Forces of Chaos, I dedicate the cello and the viola—our first prizes!" Jedermann spread his cape the width of the stage.

The flames licked closer to the cello, when suddenly Tyler raced through the dark arches leading into the courtyard with the others right behind him. Erkenbald blared the four-note signal to the gnomes over and over. Tyler blasted the dotted rhythm of the fugue as he ran. In horror he saw the flames flare within inches of Leonard's cello—and Antonio holding the torch.

These will not be the last steps I take, Tyler said to himself. He ran headlong toward the heap of instruments. Erkenbald signaled for the other gnomes, who emerged from the tunnels and jumped down from a distant turret. He continued his signal at full force and flew through the air toward the heap of burning wood. He played powerfully while the other gnomes leaped from the air to surround the now smoking bonfire, blowing their piccolos.

Jedermann spotted Tyler running toward the fire with the others. His body jerked as though a powerful electrical shock had shot through him. "How could you let this happen!" he screamed at his top Seirens. "Seize them, you fools! Seize them!"

Amathes and Aplestos swooped toward the gnomes, but the high tones of their piccolos sent them flying backwards, smashing into the wall.

Leonard and the others joined Tyler by the fire, scrambling, trying to dodge Seirens, looking for their sacred instruments, unable to see them through the flames and smoke.

"Antonio," Tyler yelled. "Wake up!" He blasted the fugal flute as loudly as he could into Antonio's face. He thought he saw a flicker of recognition.

At that moment a powerful saber-tooth Seiren grabbed Christina, holding her over the flames, ready to toss her in. Antonio's head snapped and in the brief second he locked eyes with Christina, she spoke to him with her soul.

You are not one of them. You're one of us.

Her thoughts were relentless. They drove through his mind like flashes of lightening.

You were meant for good, to bring balance—and peace—not chaos.

And at the very moment the first flame singed Christina's foot, Antonio's spell was broken. With one hand he grabbed her away from the Seiren, with the other he raised his torch menacingly.

Jedermann screamed and pointed the Baton at him, "Set your friend on fire! Now!"

"No!" Tyler yelled. Christina stared into Antonio's eyes, willing his next move.

Antonio glared defiantly at Jedermann and tossed his torch into the flock of Seirens who'd just hurled themselves at Tyler's feet. Their wings caught on fire. They flew frantically away, trying to put out the flames. Antonio set Christina down and dashed into the smoking pile of flames to grab his drum.

"Antonio!" Tyler cheered. "You're back!"

Antonio jumped to the ground and raised his drum in triumph, coughing from the smoke.

Leonard dove headfirst into the fire, reaching for Tyler's horn. He somehow knew he would be unharmed as he pulled it out and threw it to Tyler. Leonard then spotted his cello, almost engulfed in flames. He lunged for it, singeing his arms and clothes, but the second his hands touched the cello, the flames were extinguished, the instrument shone good as new, and his scorched skin was healed.

"Another miracle!" Tyler proclaimed.

Leonard smiled and raised the bow of his cello, exploding into the lowest voice of the fugue, joining his friends in music. The fire raged now but it didn't matter. His reunion with his cello felt greater than anything he'd ever experienced. Tyler joined him, playing on his long lost horn.

"STOP THEM!" Jedermann screamed.

Kathy ran toward her viola. Aplestos blocked her way and hissed into her face. "You're going to ruin your fancy clothes! You'll get filthy, you little witch! Wouldn't you rather have another jewel?" She held out a sparkling emerald.

"Out of my way!" she yelled in Aplestos' face and grabbed the viola before it was swallowed in flames.

"Way to go, Kathy!" Leonard yelled.

Kathy's heart leaped. She smiled and jumped away from the fire and smoke, breaking the heel off one of her boots. She shrugged and pulled the heel off her other one. Her blouse turned black in the flying ashes. "I've got it! I've got it!" she cheered, holding up the viola, her smudged face beaming. She turned to Aplestos and launched into the dotted rhythm of the fugue. The Seiren recoiled and raised her wings, barely lifting off before falling to the ground.

Jedermann raised the baton higher, shaking his fist in anger. A tremendous clap of thunder roared through the air. Gale force wind blasted the courtyard, shooting sparks everywhere and knocking over many Seirens and children, but not Dr. Fuddle's army of five, who stood playing their hearts out on their very own sacred instruments.

Amathes flew toward Aplestos, trying to help her, but the music played so harmoniously, so powerfully, that both Seirens were weakened, trembling.

"ARRRGGGHHHH!" Amathes flipped in violent somersaults into the fire.

Leonard's cello raged into its fortissimo eighth notes, colliding with Kathy's triplets, producing a frightening explosion. For the first time in her life, her music filled her with unsurpassed passion.

Jedermann raised his baton and lifted Amathes out of the fire with its thrust.

The gnomes landed on the backs of more of the Seirens and tooted their piccolos loudly into their ears, sending them sailing through the air, thrashing like savage beasts. They held on tightly to the Seirens, playing their instruments full blast to knock them right and left away from Tyler, Christina, and the others.

Aplestos spotted Dolly hanging loosely in Christina's arm and reveled in the opportunity for an act of sheer revenge. She gathered her strength to fly toward Christina, yanking Dolly away from her. Christina reached for her in vain. Aplestos shot her a searing cat look as she threw her Dolly into the flames. Christina panicked, unable to get to her doll. The flames licked at Dolly's feet. Tyler ran, kicking his way over burning embers to Dolly's side. Aplestos yowled then grabbed Tyler's ankle. Amathes crawled to her side to try to help her.

Leonard raised his bow with even greater determination, forcefully sweeping into the cello's thrusting rhythms. "Hear this!"

At the sounds of the cello, Amathes hissed, crippled, unable to hold onto Tyler. At that instant, Kathy applied her bow to her viola, attacking the notes with superhuman gusto. She reached for Christina and pulled her away from the pile of flames and smoke, but Dolly was no longer visible.

"Back off!" Kathy screamed to Aplestos and Amathes.

The power of her playing combined with Leonard's caused Amathes to roar like the tiger he was. He writhed and twisted, then barely managed to take off.

Tyler saw the look of terror in Christina's eyes. "I'll save

Dolly, Christina. Stay with Antonio!" He spotted Dolly. The bottom of her foot had caught on fire. He paid no attention to the flickering flames and reached for the doll.

Chapter Twenty-Three

"I'VE GOT HER, CHRISTINA!" Tyler held Dolly high in the air as he ran toward her.

Seeing her doll safe in her brother's hand, Christina's eyes brightened.

When Kathy saw two Seirens ready to pounce on Tyler, she struck her bow against the strings of her viola with such thunderous force they flew off.

Tyler pushed through the mob with Dolly, delivering her into Christina's welcoming arms. He gazed upon Christina's face and smiled with hope as she hugged Dolly and stared up into the air. He knew that look. He'd seen it many times. She'd heard something the others hadn't.

"Fight them, you bumbling idiots!" Jedermann's face blazed brighter than the flames as he shouted to the Seirens, but the power of the fugue drowned out his voice. He raised his cloak high to shield himself. "Just kill them now! Kill all of them and be done with this!"

Kathy turned her head and paused to listen. She heard it, too.

The sound of violins.

She looked at Christina whose smile danced across her lips.

Antonio and Leonard heard the sounds coming from beyond the courtyard walls and joy overtook their blackened faces. Antonio beamed at the others.

"I know that music. I know it! That's our Rachmaninoff Concerto!"

Their hearts swelled with the familiar notes. Jedermann's drummers were pounding irregularly and loudly, but many of Orphea's youth noticed the other music. For the first time in ages hope danced in their eyes. The ground shook as the sounds outside the courtyard increased.

The louder the music played, the fiercer the havoc grew among the Seirens. They crashed into one another, falling into the fire, burning, howling, cursing and trying to roll out of the way of the flames.

Then Jedermann cracked the baton like a whip and shot fire from his eyes using a force so deadly it would seem impossible to survive. At the very moment Tyler went to blow his horn, the power of the flames from Jedermann's eyes froze Tyler's body into place.

"I can't move!" he screamed.

And then with another powerful blow Jedermann raised the baton, snapped it at Christina and shot more flames from his eyes. She also froze into place, with Dolly in her arms.

Kathy raced toward Christina, but it was too late. Jedermann performed the same force on Kathy, whipping the baton at her ankles and she, too, was unable to move. "Christina!" she shouted in vain.

Within seconds Jedermann had frozen Antonio and Leonard as well, stopping all the music in his courtyard with the power of his might. He roared victoriously while his Seirens recovered and began to dance. The children of Orphea dared not move but watched in horror.

The music from outside the courtyard dramatically

increased in volume, and once reaching the critical sound level, the captive young people began to move. One by one they reached for the hundreds of instruments scattered on the ground, joining in the growing concerto rhythms of the advancing army of sound.

Jedermann, with Amathes and Aplestos behind him, realized the ranks were beginning to swell against him. A bolt of fear shook Jedermann's heart of coal. His own abductees were marching against him now. The power of their music unfroze Christina first, then Tyler and the others who immediately launched into their parts of the concerto they'd been taught by Dr. Fuddle and their composer instructors.

Kathy smiled at Leonard. "I'm thinking about those rose petals, aren't you?" she said, beaming with joy.

"Yes," Leonard shouted. "YES!"

Jedermann looked as though he would burst from anger. "Protect me, you fools! Orphea belongs to me!" he screamed to Amathes and Aplestos.

"It's too late, Master!" Aplestos said.

"We're doomed, DOOOOMED!" Amathes showed himself for the coward that he was.

"NOOOOOOOOOOOOOOOOO!" Jedermann screamed with all his strength, flailing the baton into the air, but to no avail. Even the fire could no longer shoot from his eyes.

Then it seemed that Tyler, Christina and all in the courtyard noticed it at once.

The baton began to twitch in Jedermann hands. He lost control of its movement. The power of the oncoming music began to possess the baton.

"FIGHT THEM!" Jedermann roared, sweat drenching his face.

With ever increasing tension, the sounds of tympani overpowered all the other sounds in the air.

Brrrooom, Brrrooom, Brrrooom erupted the beating drums, like a volcano ready to blow. Louder and louder grew the music, approaching the gate of the courtyard.

Brrrooom, Brrrooom, Brrrooom the tones pounded. Jedermann's drummers joined in the percussive assault.

Brrrooom, Brrrooom, Brrrooom! With each beat, the music mounted in volume, an unstoppable force for good. The Seirens throughout the courtyard flapped their wings, but the might of the music forced them to cease their wails.

Then the ground shook violently, as in a powerful earth-quake. Jedermann glared in defiance at his Seirens below, who were filled with awe at the sounds overtaking the scene. They danced away from the flames and into the midst of Orphea's best young musicians, who were spinning round and round.

Antonio cheered. "We can overcome! No doubt about it." He pounded his drum to the exact beat he'd been taught by Dr. Fuddle. Tyler and his friends raised their instruments victoriously.

At that very instant a resounding thud shook the ground outside the courtyard's massive gates. The unmistakable bass notes of a piano crashed through the air. Christina raised Dolly high into the air.

"Did I hear a piano?" Kathy asked.

"Yes!" answered voices from all directions.

After an abrupt pause, the tympani players trilled their drums, rolling the sounds of the concerto toward Jedermann's walls. And then, the music exploded into one loud, sustained and furious chord.

Above the roar of the drums and the intense chord, the approaching thunder outside the walls grew louder until the massive wooden gate began to buckle and splinter to the sounds of a tremendous outburst of octaves.

Jedermann lifted his head high, refusing to surrender.

192

Amathes and Aplestos stood by his side for the last standoff.

With a tremendous crack the gates burst open. The walls of the courtyard crumbled, casting chunks of stone onto the ground. One of the five giant turrets fell onto the burning fire, extinguishing it with one loud crash. The walls completely gave way.

Christina was the first to catch the sight of the Orphean troops as they plowed through the wreckage. The army, led by a commander on top of a mighty machine, rolled over the rubble, with an ocean of Orphea's citizens playing their instruments in its wake. Children tooted their small flutes along with the gnomes.

And then, low and behold, the greatest sight of all.

On top of the rolling platform sat a musician at his piano, pounding the keys exuberantly. Rachmaninoff stood behind him conducting the other musicians.

Tyler and Christina pointed, looking at their friends, unable to believe their eyes. "Could it be?" Tyler asked. He took a closer look at the commander playing the piano with the general's hat perched on his head.

"It is, because it must be!" Leonard shouted. "That's Dr. Fuddle up there!"

"He's alive!" Antonio and Kathy shouted, bursting with joy. "HE'S ALIVE!"

"And he's playing his own piano!" Tyler yelled.

"It CAN'T be!" Jedermann screamed.

Christina clapped wildly, waving to Dr. Fuddle.

Tyler and Antonio whooped in uncontrolled joy, waving their instruments high into the air.

"The reinforcements have arrived!" Dr. Fuddle shouted. His voice was unmistakable. His face was radiant with light and his white robe flowed with sound. "Move the forces behind the five young musicians on the front lines. Follow the

Messengers of Music!"

"Close in on the enemy!" Rachmaninoff commanded the troops.

"Now to reclaim the Gold Baton!" Dr. Fuddle flashed a smile, broad and joyous. "I knew you'd be here, our courageous Messengers of Music. The Prophecy will be fulfilled." He beamed at Tyler. "Now lead us to victory!"

The friends watched figures dressed in full armor with cellos move rapidly into place. Thick steel covered their bodies and their chest plates were decorated with bold musical symbols. Neck guards and helmets protected them from their shoulders up, but clearly visible were the familiar faces of the inhabitants underneath. Bach, Mozart and Liszt smiled at them through their helmet visors—and alongside was another man, whose noble face shone with the unmistakable brilliance of victory.

"Look! I can't believe it!" Kathy shouted. "It's Beethoven!"

Jedermann flew frantically around the courtyard attempting to revitalize his dying Seirens and bully the fleeing Seirens into staying with him.

Amathes and Aplestos glared at the Messengers of Music leading the musical army and summoned one last burst of energy. They flew toward the Messengers.

"That's the last sight you'll ever see!" Aplestos screamed, going for Kathy's throat.

"That's what you think!" yelled another girl, blasting her viola in Aplestos' ears. She let go of Kathy, enraged, and flew off to prepare to attack again.

Then Kathy saw her rescuer. "Johanna!" she cried. Soon all of Bach's children surrounded the five Messengers, marching toward Jedermann. Others joined in.

"We're right with you," Elizabeth and Juliet shouted, keeping Aplestos restrained with their violins.

"We'd never let you down!" Johann Christoph said to Leonard, proudly joining him, the two cellos performing loud, half notes in unison, driving Amathes away. Other Bach brothers blended their double basses with Antonio's rhythms. Christina blew her flute beside Tyler as he played his French horn. All of Bach's children and the Messengers of Music marched together united; moving closer and closer toward their enemy, while Amathes and Aplestos retreated back to Jedermann's side. The rising of the last movement of Rachmaninoff's *Third Concerto* grew so strong that Seirens, one by one, blended into a mighty chorus, joining Rachmaninoff's musical score.

The remaining Seirens who wouldn't surrender and harmonize, hissed and roared in pain, while their skin dissolved and their veins dangled, until they disintegrated into ashes.

"We've still got a war to win!" Tyler shouted. The friends held their instruments high, proudly marching as the front line of commanding officers in the musical army.

The piano concerto soared into the air. Dr. Fuddle played powerful double major chords while the full orchestra supported each mighty surge of sound. Clarinets doubled their voices in octaves along with trumpets. The unstoppable warriors of Orphea proceeded relentlessly toward the stage.

Jedermann stood strong, powerful, with no thought of surrendering. Only Amathes and Aplestos, who had shape-shifted into three times their size, remained at his side.

The musicians marched onward while cymbals crashed and the strains of strings soared behind the piano. With each crescendo the tempo of the music accelerated, advancing the army closer and closer toward Jedermann. All his former victims now joined the ranks of the army of fellow Orpheans, intent upon their freedom, upon Jedermann's downfall. Thousands more villagers joined the march as far as the eye could see, blowing upon their flutes. As the musicians reached the stage, the music seemed as though it were flying through the air, suspended on a giant, invisible shield.

With each musical pulse of the marching army, the gnomes danced furiously with their piccolos, bouncing off the piano and leaping through the air with joy.

Jedermann glared at the onslaught of the forces moving toward him. He signaled to Amathes and Aplestos, who flew off and came back within minutes, each leading a fresh army of hundreds of Seirens, pouring out of the tunnels, ready to do battle.

The composers nodded to each other while Dr. Fuddle raised his hand to manifest even more platoons of warriors and villagers. The music had built up such a mighty force of power, even the new Seiren reinforcements joined in song the moment they entered the field of vibration. Over and over the chords thundered through the air, transforming the remains of Jedermann's army with life-changing harmonies, one after another.

Jedermann watched in fury as his entire new army of Seirens left their positions to scurry away or join the Orphean musicians. And when that dust had settled, only Jedermann remained, with Amathes and Aplestos backed against the courtyard wall, bearing their fangs.

Mozart smiled broadly, signaling with his bow for the composers' four cellos to split into two parts—Beethoven taking the upper voice with him, while Bach and Liszt took the lower voice. The composers drew back their bows and pounced onto a tremendous chord with Dr. Fuddle leaping into action on his piano. Amathes and Aplestos shrieked as the musicians performed one great chord after another.

And then, Dr. Fuddle's machine rolled onto the stage. He leaned over his piano to come face to face for the last time with Jedermann.

"Your days were numbered, Jedermann!" he declared. "You could have chosen greatness!"

Jedermann collapsed to his knees, the blackened baton clutched to his breast.

What happened next seemed as though in slow motion:

At the very moment the music swelled to its greatest grandeur, to that powerful double E-flat Major chord from Dr. Fuddle's own hands, the sounds—the very notes themselves—took physical shape as hands of light, suspending the bodies of Amathes and Aplestos into the air. And from Dr. Fuddle's fingertips on the piano along with Tyler's horn, the notes reformed into a massive beam of light that bubbled straight toward Jedermann, piercing him through his chest, bursting wide open his black heart.

The brightness of that light melted Jedermann's bones. The forceful sounds of the music began to melt his face.

Dr. Fuddle barreled onto the piano keys in a thunderous upward sweep.

Tyler blew his horn with all his might.

"A A A A A H H H H H H H H H H H H H H H H H!" Jedermann's howl echoed off the mountains into the valleys, while the rest of his body and the last of his Seiren lieutenants disintegrated in the air.

The baton floated slowly into the waiting hands of Christina—turning back to bright gold when she touched it.

All that remained of Jedermann and his followers were their ashes blowing round in swirls to the sounds of the army's victorious strains.

It was over.

Jedermann and his destructive hoard remained no more. While Jedermann's final ashes fell in a heap to the ground, Dr. Fuddle concluded the concerto with one last surge of descending octaves followed by a flash of ascending chords. His hands alternated so fast they became almost invisible. With the last chord, triumph washed over the orchestra and the mass of joyous Orpheans.

Dr. Fuddle smiled at Christina, Tyler and their friends and motioned them onto the rolling piano platform. "All aboard!" Dr. Fuddle said. They hopped up and took a long bow together in response to the cheering throngs. Dr. Fuddle then guided Christina's hand in a sweeping gesture with the Gold Baton, transforming the piano machine into an elegant golden chariot, instantly transporting them all inside.

Christina waved the Gold Baton at all the children throughout the courtyard. From those closest to her to those so distant they could barely be seen, the power of her goodness sparked new music in Orphea—music that had never been heard. With a wave of the Gold Baton, young men in the distance found drums and began to play them; broken guitars were restored. Everyone smiled and laughed and danced while crowds gathered around to watch. Instruments of all shapes and sizes began to appear out of nowhere so that there was not a young person in all of Orphea who was not dancing or singing or playing an instrument.

And at that moment, Tyler knew his courage had given Christina the very gift his mother had wanted for her—her voice through music.

Dr. Fuddle saluted the composers, the Messengers of Music and all the victors. "A job well done, all. A job well done!"

"A truly commanding performance of the finest magnitude!" Bach said.

"Yes," Liszt agreed. "Definitely the finest use of the piano I've ever witnessed!"

"Fate has ruled once and for all in the favor of Excellence," Beethoven said, with refined authority—the composer most revered for overcoming hardship, the man who had overcome Fate.

"I tell you, I was never worried at all," laughed Mozart, winking.

The people of Orphea watched the bright rays of the sun burst through the dark clouds to embrace Dr. Fuddle and the Messengers. He then turned to the gnomes, his eyebrows raised, signaling with a salute that they had done an excellent job indeed. Then, with a mighty *WHOOSH*, the golden chariot rose into the air.

"THAT WAS SPECTACULAR!" Tyler exclaimed

Everyone aboard the golden chariot, flying high across the sky of Orphea, joined Tyler in glorious harmony with their instruments. The valley sprung forth flowers of all shapes and sizes—in hues of red, blue, violet, green, purple, white, lavender.

Christina proudly carried her symbol of strength—the symbol of her "voice" being heard—and with each wave of her Gold Baton, Orphea was fully restored with its lush fertile valleys, wide winding rivers, immense forests as far as the eye could see. Even the trees and the flowers and the plants and all the animals of Orphea joined in the joyful song. Under her Gold Baton's command, the villages returned miraculously to their former glory. The people of Orphea were healed. They ran underneath the golden chariot, waving and cheering and making music.

Now was the time for a celebration of a glorious new age for Orphea.

Chapter Twenty-Four

"I've never seen musicians more prepared for a performance," Dr. Fuddle declared. He smiled broadly and looked at his pupils, who had indeed proven themselves to be Orphea's long-awaited Messengers of Music.

They surrounded him in the vast backstage of the mighty Olympus outdoor theater, ready for their victory performance, holding their instruments with unsurpassed pride. The Albrechtsberger Conservatory Instrumental Craftsmen had inspected each instrument, carefully polishing them to make sure they were in top condition for the performance. Christina couldn't stop staring at the Gold Baton in her small hand, hardly able to believe that it was hers to hold.

Dr. Fuddle put his hands on the shoulders of his brave soldiers. "I'm sorry you had to go through the pain of being left all alone on the bridge. Do you understand why it had to happen that way?"

"We had to learn we had the power within us," Tyler said. "And that we could do it by ourselves." The others affirmed his answer with their expressions.

Dr. Fuddle was greatly pleased.

Countess Thun stepped backstage to greet the Messengers. "How nice all of you look!" She had personally taken it upon herself to see to it that they had been groomed after the battle and dressed in the finest robes of Orphea by her best clothiers.

"I can't get over this dress!" Kathy said, admiring her deep red billowing gown. The top consisted of three layers of matching silk with black ribbons tied to both sides of the narrow cut waist. "My mother would be beside herself!" The skirt was made up of brilliant red layers of matching silk satin. A black brocade petticoat peeked out from under the bottom layers.

The girls surrounded Christina for another look at her gown, which was the grandest of all. Its base was a deep earthen green with wide floral patterned panniers—side hoops, and an underskirt with seven rows of gathered ruffles. The sleeves, adorned with three layers of Chantilly lace accents, ended in narrow cuffs. The short train had embroidered golden floral patterns.

The boys looked equally stunning. Leonard in his dark red coat with wide cuffs over a long black brocade waistcoat and black breeches was a perfect match with Kathy's gown. Tyler and Antonio wore long collared tan coats with ivory embroidered silk vests and brown velvet breeches. All five of them had had their hair washed, dried, and were adorned with powdered wigs. They'd even been given manicures.

"Don't you ever dare tell my friends back home about this part!" Antonio joked, knocking Tyler on the shoulder with his fist.

As for the Messengers themselves, the thrill of victory had given them a sense of confidence second to none. Even their speech had changed as they assumed their new roles as the honored heroes and heroines of Orphea—the ones who would be known forever as saving the realm from sure doom.

"You've made me so proud, my pupils, my friends," Dr. Fuddle said, his voice faltering. "It is nearly impossible for me to contain my joy."

The Messengers peered from behind the thick red velvet curtain, which stood between them and the stage of the amphitheatre teeming with throngs of musicians. They could hear the last minute preparations for the performance. The backdrop looked like a spread of angels' wings fanning over the top, curling around both sides.

Throngs of villagers gathered in the region below. They'd come from all directions, dressed in stylish clothing, taking their seats in the outdoor amphitheater that gave sweeping views of the stage.

"This may well be the grandest performance we've ever heard!" said a woman, wearing a deep burgundy velvet corset top with matching skirt.

"I just can hardly wait to see the little girl with the Gold Baton," said her friend. "That Orphea has been spared is nothing short of a miracle."

Others around them spoke with deepest gratitude of having their children back and their villages and lives fully restored.

Dr. Fuddle led the Messengers closer to the edge of the curtain to get a better view of the stage of polished marble, much like they'd seen all over Orphea.

"Look who's coming," Dr. Fuddle said excitedly. "It's the extraordinary man who single-handedly changed the entire course of music history. He knew his mission even as a child. He was in tune with his destiny all along."

"It's Beethoven!" Kathy said, overcome by the sight of her favorite composer joining them backstage.

They watched in awe as Ludwig van Beethoven walked toward them.

"I've never had such an honor," Beethoven said humbly, bowing graciously.

After everything they'd seen in Orphea, nothing swept them off their feet more than being in the close company of Beethoven.

"You are now eyewitnesses, dear ones," he said, "that the Universe brings together those who are chosen according to its great purpose."

Beethoven smiled at each Messenger, knowing that every one of them had been vitally necessary for victory—each playing the role they were destined to play. He opened his arms wide to receive them into his embrace. He set Christina apart from the others. "And now you, young lady, may have learned the greatest lessons of all."

Dr. Fuddle cherished the tender moment, watching the light dance in Christina's eyes.

"It is a lesson I had to learn, too, that no handicap is too great to prevent one's voice from being heard."

"A great lesson, indeed!" Dr. Fuddle declared. He beamed at his pupils and knew the time had come. "This is it, my young friends." He smiled at them one last time and turned to Beethoven. "It's time to perform."

Soon a collective hush overtook the multitude of spectators and musicians. Beethoven walked onto the platform, taking his seat at Dr. Fuddle's piano, directly in front of the orchestra. The throng cheered as he took a small bow and positioned himself. There was an air of divinity in his every move.

When Dr. Fuddle led the Messengers from behind the curtains onto the stage a roaring thunder of applause greeted them. Their hearts pounded with excitement. Christina held the Gold Baton in one hand and her brother's hand in the other. Dolly was neatly tucked in one of her fancy pockets.

The roars of applause, the cheers for Dr. Fuddle and the

Messengers of Music, seemed like they would never cease. Beethoven and the musicians rose to their feet and saluted Dr. Fuddle when he stepped forward.

"Greetings, ladies and gentlemen, honored guests and fellow lovers of music." Dr. Fuddle's voice echoed across the amphitheater. "Please be seated." The concertgoers settled into their seats. "I stand here today before a victorious people. A people who have seen their land saved from the ravages of mediocrity, disharmony, and corruption—a land whose children were once endangered by one of the darkest of forces in known history. And I'm proud to say with utter assurance to everyone within the sound of my voice: the light of harmony has destroyed our enemy."

The spectators rose to their feet again, cheering. The men raised their fists in victory and the ladies hugged one another, smiling. Children danced with gnomes in the aisles before everyone settled into their seats once more.

"Today we honor this victory," Dr. Fuddle said, "with a very special performance of Beethoven's *Choral Fantasy* for piano, orchestra, chorus and soloists with our very own esteemed, beloved composer Herr Ludwig van Beethoven, pianist, along with the Orphea Chorus and Orchestra and our very special guest performers, the Messengers of Music.

"Each one of these five young people brought to us their own strengths. We couldn't be here without a single one of them. It was their faith, passion, courage, and dedication that brought about this momentous victory. And I now proudly present them to you."

Tyler took a deep breath and clutched his French horn. Antonio looked at his drum already set in the percussion section, which had transformed into a mighty set of tympani. Kathy adjusted her glasses and checked her dress one last time.

"Kathy Goldman, viola." She bowed and took her place as principal violist with the others in her row. A loud round of applause greeted each of them while they took their positions in the orchestra.

"Leonard Lang, cello." The crowd shouted approval as he took his seat.

"Antonio Romero, tympani." Young men in the audience cheered "Antonio, Antonio!" as he took his place.

"And Tyler Harrington, French horn." Tyler was greeted with stomps of cheers from all the young people, shouting "Tyler, Tyler, Tyler!" as he took his position with the brass.

The soloists from their original welcome at Countess Thun's palace stood regally with the other soloists.

Juliet and Elizabeth were seated in the front row of violinists, giving their friends a look of approval.

Only Christina remained standing with Dr. Fuddle.

"And now, ladies and gentlemen, I present to you our very, very special guest conductor. She will be known throughout history for her love of great music. Yes, ladies and gentlemen, our very own—Christina Harrington!"

Beethoven rose to his feet first, quickly followed by the orchestra and chorus members while the entire multitude cheered for Christina. She performed a deep bow, remaining next to Dr. Fuddle.

He cleared his throat before continuing. "It is through this young lady that the forces of Good have graced us and with the combined efforts of the Messengers of Music, the prophecy has been fulfilled. And in the words written by the esteemed poet, Christoph Kuffner, specifically for this masterpiece we will perform today, I quote:

"When love and strength are united, harmony rewards Man."

Dr. Fuddle waited for the applause to finish and led Christina by the hand to her place at the conductor's podium. He smiled tenderly at her and whispered in her ear: "Music begins where language ends, my dear."

Dr. Fuddle walked across the stage and climbed a small

staircase to a special box seat reserved for him along with the Countess and other royal dignitaries for full view of Christina, Beethoven, and all the musicians.

Christina felt chills energize her body. As she watched Dr. Fuddle taking his seat, his radiant face brought an inspiration that would last forever in her mind. His immortal words sank deeply and forever into her heart and her soul. She held the Gold Baton high toward the musicians before pointing it to Beethoven. She'd studied the movements of the conductors in Orphea, memorizing their every move without anyone noticing.

Christina Harrington

Beethoven watched Christina closely. After a brief silence, she signaled with the Baton. He raised his left hand, and crashed it thunderously onto the piano keys, joined immediately by his right hand on another chord, followed by a burst of octaves and thirds. But something extraordinary was happening. As Christina pointed the Gold Baton at him, the musical notes issuing from his fingers took shape before the marveling eyes of all to see: they looked like kaleidoscopic bubbles, each as unique as a snowflake, filling the air with a dazzling array of prismatic spheres.

For several minutes Beethoven dazzled both fellow musicians and audience members with displays of technical fireworks. His fingers and arms moved so quickly over the keys and across the wide expanse of the piano that they appeared blurred. Soon his solo section concluded, followed by a double handed rip across the keys, a feat so forceful it looked as though he would tear the ivories off the instrument. The visible sound leapt into the air dancing as madly as the gnomes themselves.

Christina pointed the Gold Baton toward Leonard. He began a very soft, low march in the cello section, his spherical notes dark and symmetrical and enormous. Within seconds she signaled for it to stop. She motioned to Beethoven, who played a soft chord, followed by a short, single note, then an intricate right hand melody. Next she waved the Baton before Kathy. The violists and violinists imitated the march begun by the cellos, quickly, but softly as the cellists had done, followed by another, brief melody on the piano.

Finally Christina pointed to her brother Tyler. He smiled at her and his eyes sent waves of love that surrounded her. He never felt prouder of his sister. Then he blasted a short fanfare of sky-blue notes on his French horn, imitated directly by the oboes, ending on a long sustained chord, which ushered in a duet between Beethoven and the French horns. Bubbles of sound filled and refilled the air with rainbows of geometrical perfection. Within seconds there came a glittery flute solo, leading into a duet with the oboes, followed by the oboes with the piano.

Back and forth the interplay continued until only the strings performed. Dr. Fuddle was delighted, watching seven-year-old Christina conduct the orchestra like a professional— bringing music to life with the passion of a great musical genius. She led the string section, then with a sudden sweeping motion of the Gold Baton, the full orchestra exploded into action. Trumpets blasted their parts. Beethoven followed Christina's conducting precisely. His fingers raced over the piano keys, performing an elaborate display of his technique.

The performance proceeded until finally the excitement was replaced with calm, as if the musicians were given a rest before something even greater took place. Dr. Fuddle glowed with satisfaction, studying his pupils all the while. He'd never seen such looks of sheer triumph.

He watched Antonio raise his hands with the mallets, coming down with thunderous force onto the tympani, sending massive planets of magenta high into the air.

And Kathy and Leonard, how they'd transformed! Dr. Fuddle couldn't have been prouder watching them while they played, astonishing the crowd with their talent.

Then there was Tyler, the leader of the group—this special brave young man—how satisfied he looked playing that French horn.

Soon the tranquil sounds changed and the singers raised their heads high in preparation to join in the performance. The original themes of the work returned, just as they had started minutes earlier.

Suddenly Beethoven pounced upon the keys with a fiendish gaze, raising himself off the bench, momentarily airborne, before crashing back down, releasing a frenzy of thunderous notes. His intensity seemed unsurpassable when the chorus joined in to sing:

"With grace, charm and sweet sounds, the harmonies of our life, and the sense of beauty engenders the flowers, which eternally bloom!"

Dr. Fuddle was so moved by the exquisite shapes of each vocal sound he could barely contain himself.

Christina nearly floated above the musicians she conducted. Her eyes beamed with the thrill of hearing the singers bursting into action. Their voices sounded like music from all the heavens combined.

Dr. Fuddle could see his pupils were fully transformed by the power of the music. He closed his eyes, allowing himself to cherish every second, witnessing the great joy flood into the very souls of the five Messengers. He silently drank in the beauty of the moment, and began to transcend from his physical state into a state of pure love.

It seemed impossible that in the history of music there could ever be any music more wonderful than what rang out in that magnificent concert of all concerts. Nothing could compare. Dr. Fuddle felt the strength of the full chorus as they joined in melodious harmonies. Sharing this experience with the Messengers—combined with their victorious participation—caused him to marvel as never before.

When the performance neared its final moments, Beethoven unleashed his full powers. His face looked like that of a madman as he thundered and hurled his hands like a mighty god over the keys, like Zeus hurling thunderbolts off Mt. Olympus. Each chord triumphed into the air, combining with the sounds of the orchestra and singers.

By the time the performance came to its peak, the very ground trembled. The magnitude of the musical creation along with the victory, which had restored Orphea, rendered everyone unable to move or even breathe while the last note penetrated the air.

When that final tone disappeared, there was first profound silence. Then the audience leaped to its feet, collectively applauding, crying, "BRAVO, BRAVO!"

Beethoven rose, reaching for Christina's hand. He led her front and center of the stage to bow with him. The musicians and multitudes cheered while Beethoven and Christina turned to the musicians. She pointed the Gold Baton to Tyler, Antonio, Leonard and Kathy motioning them to stand to be recognized for their brilliant performances.

Dr. Fuddle's joy was beyond description, watching the audience cheer for his pupils. He felt satisfied that he'd followed his earthly calling, to reveal the greatness of music to young people. He knew that this unforgettable experience with Beethoven would forever secure the Messengers' appreciation for beauty.

And then suddenly, a great light appeared.

Christina motioned for her brother and the other Messengers to join her. They walked together with their instruments to the edge of the stage, bowing together.

One by one the musicians behind them became part of the great light. Christina and Tyler looked into the face of Dr. Fuddle, motioning him to join them, but he was disappearing into the light, along with Countess Thun.

Dr. Fuddle looked into their faces and spoke to them through his mind:

There is purpose behind the mystery of music.

Dr. Fuddle knew they could hear him.

The purpose is the passion and joy one can only feel in that precious moment when one becomes aware of it. It is that passion that joins souls together and makes us one.

Dr. Fuddle's image blended with the light and his face suddenly revealed itself—as the eternal Orpheus, god of music. Then to the astonishment of all, the face of Tyler and Christina's dear mother appeared next to him, smiling with joy.

Mrs. Harrington gazed upon her son and daughter and spoke to them, "All things are possible, now, my darlings," she said. "This is only the beginning. You were chosen to pass this joy to the next generation."

Dr. Fuddle and Mrs. Harrington began to disappear high above the clouds along with Beethoven and the singers. Soon a heavenly chorus of angels replaced the sounds of the cheering audience members, who transformed into light and rose into the sky. Their light images floated high above the children and gathered together with a mighty wind behind Dr. Fuddle. The Messengers of Music felt themselves being wafted away from the great light of Orphea.

Just before the face of Dr. Fuddle disappeared like the waning moon into the sky, his last words clearly proclaimed: "This is the day the universe has infused your souls with music! Let us rejoice, forevermore!"

And with these words, Christina pointed the Gold Baton high into the air, reaching toward the light.

But everything was gone.

211

Postlude

A few moments passed. The musical light and the angelic singing were no more.

It was Tyler who first noticed the piano back in Dr. Fuddle's music parlor in the old mansion. The moon shone through the glass.

Leonard looked around, stunned, while Kathy glanced at her watch.

"7:15," she said. "7:15?"

She checked again to make sure. Her watch had stopped.

"It stopped at 7:15! That's the exact time we first arrived here!"

Antonio stared at Tyler while Christina stood holding Dolly in one hand and Tyler's hand in the other. Leonard looked at his watch. It also said 7:15.

One by one they gazed at one another. Kathy's purse hung over her shoulder. Everyone was dressed in the clothes in which they'd arrived. They surveyed the room in utter astonishment.

The hardwood floors reflected the busts of the composers throughout the parlor and the oil portraits graced the room along with the chandeliers, just as they had all along.

"What the?" Antonio said, taking a few steps backwards.

"What….what…what happened?" was all Kathy managed to stammer.

Leonard walked across the parlor and stepped through its arched doors out into the hallway.

"This can't be!" he shouted.

But sure enough, at the end of the hallway stood the open door they had entered at exactly 7:15.

They stared dumbfounded at one another.

For several moments, no one spoke, until Tyler broke the silence. "What did I tell you about this place?" he said. "I know we trespassed, but I think it was for a good cause, don't you?"

"Yes it was." Kathy said. They all nodded in agreement.

"We can go now." Tyler smiled at his friends. "Thanks to all of you, I've accomplished what I was meant to do. Now we all have a mission to celebrate music." He looked behind the piano to the wall where the Golden Doors had stood. "I believe we're always welcome here."

"How can we be sure this even happened?" Leonard asked.

Antonio was standing at the window. "Take a look," he pointed.

The friends turned to look—and saw the night sky was splendid with stars.

"His canopy of stars is restored," Tyler pronounced.

He led the others, speechless, out of the music parlor. But before stepping across the threshold, Christina spotted a large, elevated glass case no one had noticed before. She pointed.

In it were four instruments—a viola, a cello, a French horn and a snare drum—and right in the middle, on a small stand of its own, a beautiful relic with a simple inscription shining beneath it that read:

THE GOLD BATON
Music Begins Where Language Ends

Glossary of Musical Terms

a cappella: *without accompaniment.*

alto: *the lowest female singing voice.*

baritone: *a low male singing voice between tenor and bass.*

bass: *the lowest male singing voice.*

bravura: *skill and virtuosity.*

carillons à musique: *musical bells.*

chamber orchestra: *a small orchestra of about two dozen players.*

chords: *three or more notes sounded simultaneously.*

chromatic scale: *a scale composed of twelve half steps.*

concerto: *a musical piece for solo instrument(s) and orchestra.*

consonance: *sounds that are pleasing to the ear.*

contrapuntal: *music which incorporates two or more melodies
        at the same time.*

counterpoint: *two or more musical lines, or melodies, performed
        simultaneously.*

dissonance: *sounds that are unpleasant to the ear.*

fanfare: *a prelude or opening usually played by brass instruments.*

forte: *loud or strong.*

fortissimo: *very loud or strong.*

fugue: *a contrapuntal piece in which two or more parts are layered
        on a recurring theme*

harmony: *the structure, progression and relationships of chords, or
        musical tones sounding at the same time; when pitches
        are in agreement.*

hertz: *a unit of measurement for frequency equal to one complete
        cycle per second.*

intervals: *the distance between two notes.*

215

lyre: *an ancient Greek instrument with a four-sided frame, encompassing strings attached from a sound box to a cross bar. Played like a harp.*

lyricism: *in a singing matter.*

maestro: *master, teacher, conductor.*

major scale: *a diatonic scale in which the half steps occur between the third and fourth, seventh and eighth notes.*

melody: *an organized sequence of single notes; the "tune."*

minuet: *a French dance from the mid-1600s in slow 3/4 time.*

musical notation: *written music indicating pitch and rhythm.*

octave: *the interval between the first and the eighth notes of the diatonic scale.*

percussionist: *a musician who plays instruments made from sonorous material that produce sounds of definite or indefinite pitch when shaken or struck, including drums, rattles, bells, gongs and xylophones.*

reed: *a vibrating strip of metal or cane, which when activated by air produces a tone.*

rhythm: *a pattern of long and short note values in music.*

scale: *a progression of notes in a specific order.*

seconds: *the interval between two consecutive notes of the diatonic scale.*

soprano: *the highest female voice.*

string quartet: *an instrumental group consisting of two violins, viola and cello.*

tenor: *a high male voice between alto and baritone.*

theme: *the musical subject of a piece, usually a melody.*

thirds: *the interval of three diatonic scale notes.*

tonic: *the first note of the scale; the keynote.*

tune: *the melody, usually the progression of musical tones that can be sung.*

tritone: *the interval of an augmented (raised) fourth or diminished (lowered) fifth; usually perceived as a very eerie, unsettling sound.*

Acknowledgements

Many special people have been helpful in the writing of the endless drafts of this book. First, I owe a debt of gratitude to Dr. Kenneth Atchity, my literary manager and friend, for seeing the potential in this story upon hearing my "pitch" for the first time at "Write the World in Atlanta" and for his consummate skills and connections in helping me coordinate my whole vision with integrity for the entire franchise. You are an amazing man! I deeply admire you as a teacher, scholar, visionary, intellectual and human being.

Next, I would like to thank two very special women: first, my very dear friend, writing coach and spiritual teacher, Mardeene Mitchell. Thank you, Mardeene, for rescuing Dr. Fuddle from his hiding place in the drawer, for prophesying this would be the project that would launch my career, for all your patience working with me on draft after draft of this book and also for introducing me to Dr. Kenneth Atchity at your conference. And second, I thank my adult piano student of many years, Karen Hargate, for introducing me to Mardeene and for your incredible spiritual perspective. Both of you women mean the world to me.

Also, I'd like to recognize and thank our "Junior

Consultants" from the target age group, who read my manuscript and answered a lengthy questionnaire. Your comments and suggestions were a very important part of this process. Their names are: Ryan Eck, Annika Grabers, Jessie Jensen, Edward McKenna, Meggie McKenna, Grayson McMichael, James Robertson and Nolan Windham. And big thanks also goes to Donna and Barri Burtch for creating artwork and design work to match my vision precisely.

I'd also like to extend special thanks to Robert Callaci, who has been a great friend, advisor and my original "fan" since 1998, when I first created and introduced Dr. Fuddle in a children's play entitled *The Magic Piano*. Your encouragement and enthusiasm were greatly appreciated from day one.

I also thank all my piano students and their parents for years of support. And of course, without the encouragement and support of my true band of friends, those who read early versions of this book and offered their suggestions and encouragement—Maniya Barredo, Rosemary Brumby, Virginia Callaci, Buddy Crawford, Melanie Cutini, Janet D'Addario, Gael Drew, Daniel Easton, Dr. Arlene Ganem, Saundra Grace, Rosi Grunschlag, Liz Harrison, Dr. David Jacobson, Gary and Anita Martin, Magin Maseda, Rhonda Matthesen, Joe Orr, Linda Stern, Jo Ann Sulcer, Eric Travena, and to the "dinner club"—Dr. Fuddle would not be ready to take the stage today.

Lastly, a very special thank you goes to Joseph DeBlasi, who has been by my side during this whole process, through thick and thin. And to my father, Jack Woodruff, for his unconditional love.

Dr. Warren L. Woodruff
drfuddlesmusicalblog.com
October 13, 2011

About the author

Dr. Woodruff was born in Indianapolis, Indiana and currently lives and teaches in Atlanta, Georgia. He holds Bachelor's and Master's degrees in Piano Performance and a Ph.D. in Musicology with a concentration in Piano Performance.

Dr. Woodruff is available world-wide for lectures, seminars and master classes. His specialties include presentations for children entitled "Meet the Composers with Dr. Woodruff" and a two-day seminar for all ages entitled "The Classical Music Crash Course."

For more information,
email drwarrenwoodruff@comcast.net.

This book is dedicated in loving memory of
Marilyn Woodruff (1934-2008).
I owe my passion for great music and literature to you.

Made in the USA
Charleston, SC
29 June 2012